AN **AMERICAN GHOST** THRILLER

REQUIEM

OTHER TITLES BY J. B. TURNER

American Ghost Series

Rogue

Reckoning

Jon Reznick Series

Hard Road

Hard Kill

Hard Wired

Hard Way

Hard Fall

3

J. B. TURNER

AN **AMERICAN GHOST** THRILLER

REQUIEM

f THOMAS & MERCER

Published by Thomas & Mercer, Seattle

www.apub.com

Amazon, the Amazon logo, and Thomas & Mercer are trademarks of Amazon.com, Inc., or its affiliates.

ISBN-13: 9781503948235
ISBN-10: 1503948234

Cover design by @blacksheep-uk.com

Printed in the United States of America

To my sons

One

The dive bar was dead.

Nathan Stone was nursing a cold beer as John Lee Hooker's "Boom Boom" growled out of the jukebox. Fox News on the TV, an off-duty Miami cop staring into his whiskey, the pink neon sign in the shape of a woman flashing on and off. A blond wearing a red bikini was asleep on the pool table. A guy in a Hawaiian shirt was talking to himself in the corner.

Stone zoned out as a reporter talked about a shooting outside a Chicago nightclub. He tasted the residue of the steroid-and-amphetamine pill he had crunched earlier.

He was thinking of calling it a night when a thirtysomething woman in killer heels sauntered into the bar alone. She looked a lot like his sister. The resemblance was uncanny.

Stone watched the woman in the mirror behind the bar. She wore skinny jeans and a tight-fitting crop top.

She pulled up a stool two down from Stone. Shifted in her seat as she tucked her long auburn hair behind her ears. Her eyes were hooded, as if she was already loaded. She ordered a bottle of Presidente beer with a tequila chaser. She drank them both in the blink of an eye.

"Same again, *Pedro*," she said to the bartender. Loudly, so she could be heard over the driving beat and guitar riffs.

"My name's not Pedro, ma'am," he said.

"What does it matter? Same again."

The bartender poured her a second tequila shot. Slid it across the bar next to another chilled bottle of Presidente.

She drank them both. When the jukebox fell silent, she turned and stared at Stone. "You from around here, honey?" she asked.

The resemblance to his soft-spoken sister vanished the moment she opened her mouth. Stone had no wish to engage her in conversation. So he just shrugged.

"It's a simple question, honey. I'm not expecting to see Stephen Hawking hanging around here, let me tell you. So, you from around here?"

"I'm in town for a few hours."

"A few hours. Is that right?" She ordered a Scotch and pointed at Stone. "Give him whatever he wants."

"I'm good, thanks," Stone said.

"I'm not asking if you're good, honey. I'm asking what you want to drink. You want a Heineken?"

Stone sighed, not wanting to get dragged into a prolonged discussion. "Heineken's good, thanks."

"Make that two Heinekens, Pedro, if you don't mind," she said.

The bartender handed them each a beer. Stone took a sip. It felt good.

The woman took two large gulps from her bottle. Led Zeppelin was now blasting out of the speakers.

"Robert Plant. What a fucking singer, right? He's English, isn't he?"

Stone nodded.

"Yeah, I thought so. So . . . you say you're in town. You at a conference?"

Stone shook his head.

"Not much of a talker, huh? Well, that's fine." She looked at the vacant stool between them. "You mind if I sit there?"

Stone shrugged. "Be my guest."

The woman smiled and slid over, swigging some beer. "My name's Justine. As in Justine time, right?" She laughed long and hard at her play on words.

Stone nursed his drink.

The woman leaned into him as she scanned the rest of the bar. "What the hell has been going on here? That girl on the pool table? Is she okay?"

"I don't know. Probably had too much to drink, I guess."

"That's very perceptive, Sherlock."

Stone shifted in his seat.

"Are you from Florida?" she asked.

Stone shook his head and took a gulp of cold beer.

"I'm from New York," she said.

"Is that right?"

"Lower East Side."

"You kidding me?" Stone said.

The woman shook her head. "Nope. Hester Street. Five of us to a room. You believe that?"

Stone smiled. He hadn't come across anyone from the Lower East Side. Ever. Apart from when he went back to the Lower East Side. "You eat at that deli?" He snapped his fingers. "You know, that famous one. Everyone in the neighborhood knows it."

She smiled sheepishly. "It's all changed these days. You wouldn't recognize it. New hotels and restaurants. Hipsters everywhere. You notice they're always talking into some cell phone or with a Bluetooth headset on? It's all messed up these days."

"What are you in town for?" Stone asked.

"Actually, I've got a modeling assignment tomorrow."

"Shouldn't you be catching up on your beauty sleep or something?"

"Too stressed. A lot of things kicking around. Bullshit manager dipping like crazy. Wants twenty-five percent of whatever I earn. You believe that? Gonna have to fire him."

Stone finished his beer and ordered two more. He pushed one toward the woman.

She raised it in a toast. "What's your name, stranger?"

"Jimmy," he said. Stone always started from the premise that no one needed to know his real name.

"Jimmy? I like it. Once dated a Jimmy. From the Village. Think he ran off with a guy who made suits for Marlon Brando back in the day."

Stone gulped his beer. Out of the corner of his eye, he saw the cop get up and leave. "Thinning out."

The woman nodded and flashed him a big smile. "You got any cocaine?"

"What?"

"I said, have you got any cocaine? What is it with people these days?"

Stone shook his head. "I don't do that stuff."

"Good for you. Wish I could give it up." She touched under her nose. "Know what my mother said?"

Stone shrugged.

"Called me a low-life little piece of shit."

"Not very sympathetic."

"Fuck her. Anyway, what does she know? Shacked up with some lubricant salesman from the Midwest. I mean, who does that?"

Stone smiled. "I have no fucking idea what you're talking about."

The woman laughed. "Well, I'm glad someone finds it funny. Me? That's my life. Stepfather sells lubricant to pharmacies across Michigan and Illinois."

"You mind changing the subject?"

The woman gave him a sly smile. "You don't like me talking about that kind of thing?"

"It's not a great icebreaker, if I'm honest."

"I don't know. We're both talking about it, right?"

Stone nodded. "Point taken."

"Hey, what are you doing for the rest of the night?"

He shrugged. "Drinking."

"What time does this place shut?"

"Five."

The woman looked around the bar and gazed at the girl in the bikini asleep on the pool table. "I'm looking for something livelier, you know what I mean?"

"Might liven up later."

"I wouldn't count on it." She leaned in close. Stone caught a whiff of cheap perfume. "Listen, you might be in luck. I'm headed to a party downtown. Friend of mine from college. She's a real scream, let me tell you."

Stone sipped some beer. "I'm not much of a party guy."

"Hey, neither am I. But I like a drink. And I can see you do too. What do you say?"

Stone looked at his watch and grimaced.

"They've got a big loft, a big-name DJ, and plenty of booze, weed, coke, or whatever you fancy."

Stone sipped some beer. He had planned to stay put for a couple more hours. He turned and looked at the woman. She was smiling.

"Come on, what's wrong with you? It'll be a blast!"

"I must be out of my mind. Sure, why the hell not?"

Stone swallowed the rest of his beer, then followed the woman out of the bar and into the alley at the side of the Deuce. A pickup truck was sitting there.

"You're gonna drive?" he said.

The woman opened the door, laughed, and slid into the driver's seat while Stone got in on the other side. She started up the engine, pulled away, weaving through the dark South Beach streets. "So, you want to party?"

Stone took his Glock from his waistband and pressed it to her head. "No, I don't want to party. I want to know the truth, you lying piece of shit."

Two

The woman swerved down Washington Avenue. "What the hell is this?" she wailed. "What are you doing?"

"Shut the fuck up and drive."

"You're scaring me. What is this? I wasn't told this was going to happen!"

Stone kept the gun trained at her head as he let the words sink in. His instincts had been correct: she was the bait in a honey trap. And that meant *they* had found him.

Not good. Not good at all.

The more he thought about it, the more he could see in terrifying clarity why the Commission had hired her. Her looks, her perfume—she resembled his sister enough to make him lower his guard but not so much as to make him suspicious. And now she was supposed to lead him to his death. They would be waiting for him. They'd torture him. Kill him.

Stone's mind was racing. He needed to keep on the move. He needed to get out of sight. She might be wearing a wire. But he also needed to find out what she knew. Decide his next move.

Stone felt the amphetamine and steroids coursing through his veins, heightening his rage and focus. He needed a plan. He needed time.

"Please don't kill me! Please, I don't want any trouble."

"Focus on the road! Get on the bridge."

The woman blinked away tears as she pulled onto the MacArthur Causeway. Ahead loomed the skyscrapers of downtown Miami.

"What's your real name?"

"Please! What have I done wrong? Where are we going?"

"You will tell me your real name, honey, or I'm going to blow your pretty little brains out. And trust me, I don't bluff."

The woman stammered. "But . . . I was told . . . Is this part of it?"

"I asked your fucking name! Real fucking name! Now!"

"Beatrice! McNally. But my stage name is Jane Chalmers."

"What the fuck are you talking about?" Stone pressed the gun hard against her neck.

"Please don't kill me! I thought . . . I was told . . . It's a job. I get paid."

"What are you talking about?"

"I'm an actress. That's all I am, I swear."

Stone realized the lengths the Commission had gone to set him up. "Why you?"

"I'm . . . I've been out of work and I'm broke. Dead broke. I was desperate for any work."

"Go on."

Tears streamed down Beatrice's face. "A Hollywood casting director called me. She said she liked the way I looked."

"Is this you acting right now?"

"No, it's not! I'm terrified."

"Tell me about this call from the casting director."

"Real nice. Sweet-talking. Thought I'd be perfect for a new film. And they gave me ten thousand dollars to fly to Miami for a casting session."

Stone contemplated what she was telling him. He was still trying to get his head around it. "You were paid to do what exactly?"

"The film was supposed to be a docudrama. Lots of improv. They told me that you would be sitting at the bar, and that you were an actor. And you were in character."

"I don't think I believe you."

"It's the truth! You think I could make shit like this up? This is too trippy for words."

Stone pressed the gun tight to her temple. "You will keep driving until I get a satisfactory answer. So you're an out-of-work actress from where exactly?"

"Santa Monica, California."

"What was the name of the casting director you spoke to?"

"I don't know. I can't remember."

"And you were given ten grand, told to go to Miami, and do what?"

"I was told to go to that bar, I was told at what time, and they described what you looked like."

Stone absorbed the information. "And you took that at face value?"

"Yes. Goddamn, I know how it looks. Makes me look like an idiot."

"Being an idiot is the least of your problems in case you hadn't noticed. How do I know you're telling the truth?"

Beatrice glanced up at a road sign. "Shit. I don't know where I am. I have no idea where I am."

"Forget about that. What were your instructions?"

"I just told you!"

"Tell me again!"

"I was told to chat you up at the Deuce bar on Fourteenth Street, say I was from the Lower East Side and all that, and then suggest going to a party in Coconut Grove."

"Pretty cute operation."

Her eyes were again filling with tears. "This wasn't my idea, I promise."

"How do I know that?"

"I'm a fucking actress! You know how much I earned last year from acting?"

"Not interested."

"Four hundred dollars. A soap voice-over. You believe that?"

But Stone's attention was locked on the side mirror. "Shut up!" he said.

Thirty yards back a Mercedes SUV was tailing them. Tinted windows, darker than was legal. With four silhouetted men inside.

Three

Stone moved the gun away from Beatrice's head as he considered his next move. "Take the ramp up ahead and get on the highway. Drive south, out of the city."

"Please," she said, "let me out."

"Not an option, honey."

Stone checked the side-view mirror again. The Mercedes SUV was still tucked in not far behind them. He didn't know for sure if it was the Commission. But if it was, they would know that she wasn't driving Stone in the direction of the party.

The more he started to plan his countermoves, the calmer he felt. More focused. The slight dulling effect of the booze had already lifted.

"So, you don't know who really contacted you?" he said. "You expect me to believe that?"

"It's the truth."

"You're an actress. What do you know about the truth? You only need to learn your lines."

Beatrice bit her lower lip as tears streamed down her face.

"Are you acting now, huh?"

"No, I'm not."

Stone glanced in the passenger-side mirror. The Mercedes was closing in. Stone felt all his senses switched on. He figured the guys tailing them—if they had indeed been sent to kill him—would be working out their next move. They would have a plan B if they were aware he'd spotted them. Of that he was sure. He wondered if Beatrice knew anything about that. But he didn't think she knew shit. Either that or she was the best actress in the world.

So the question was, Did the men in the SUV know they'd been rumbled? If Beatrice really was a clueless actress, they couldn't be certain of the reason for the detour. And so they'd be awaiting instructions to determine their next move.

He let those thoughts play out as Beatrice drove down the South Dixie Highway, past Coral Gables.

"What are you going to do with me?" she said into the silence. "Please, I've got a kid. A daughter. It's her birthday in a couple of days. I've got a party arranged for her. Please."

"Where is she now?"

"With her father. We're divorced. He got custody."

Stone glanced again in the side-view mirror. "That figures."

"What does that mean?"

"It means you're a gullible idiot, that's what."

She blinked away more tears.

"So are these tears for real or something you can produce at will?"

"Please . . . I'm scared!"

"Gimme your cell phone."

"What?"

"Just gimme it!"

"Why?"

"Listen. You're going to call the cops. And you're going to say that your ex-husband and his friend are armed and are in a black Mercedes SUV and they are following you."

Beatrice glanced in the rearview mirror. "Shit. Who are they?"

"I believe they work for the people who hired you."

"Bullshit. This is not happening."

"Pull yourself together. Here's how it's going to work. I'll give you the license plate number. You say they tried to fire at you on the highway."

"What?"

"Then you hang up."

"And if I don't?"

"Then I'll kill you myself."

Four

The car swerved as Beatrice handed Stone her cell phone. "Watch the road," he barked. He dialed 911 and pressed the cell phone to her ear.

"Don't fuck this up," he warned.

Beatrice began to cry as she gripped the wheel. "Operator, please help me! There's a black Mercedes on South Dixie Highway, headed south out of Miami. It's my ex-husband and his friend. He just shot at my car!" She turned to Stone. "License?"

Stone whispered the number to her.

Beatrice shouted it into the phone. "Please hurry! They're going to kill me!"

Stone ended the call. "You really are an actress," he said. "You did good. And you didn't fuck up. So you're gonna live."

"I appreciate that."

"At least for now." Stone glanced in the mirror, keeping an eye on the car behind them, knowing they would be considering their next move.

"You're going to kill me anyway, aren't you?"

"You'll be fine. You just need to keep doing what you're doing. You need to focus. And we'll get you through this."

"I want to get out. I want to get back to my family. This is not something I feel comfortable with."

Stone said nothing.

"Please let me out."

"By all means, not a problem. That can be arranged."

Stone opened up the back of the cell phone, took out the SIM card and battery.

"What are you doing?"

"They can't track us now via your cell phone."

Beatrice shook her head. "I want to get out. Now!"

"Keep on driving. I'll tell you when you can get out."

"Please, I can't cope with this."

"Well, we'll find out soon."

"What do you mean?"

"Drive. Eyes forward."

"Why? Are they still behind us? Where are the cops?"

"Don't freak out. Just take a breath."

Beatrice did as she was told.

"And again. Breathe in, breathe out."

She seemed about to hyperventilate; she was breathing hard and way too fast. "I can't!"

"Relax."

"Relax? How the fuck can I relax?"

"Just keep driving on this very nice highway, and just keep doing what you're told."

Beatrice went quiet as the miles flew by. A few minutes later, they both heard the wail of sirens.

Stone glanced behind them and saw two cop cars with flashing lights speed into view. They pulled the Mercedes over. "What did I tell you?"

"Okay, what now?"

"We need to get off the highway."

Beatrice took the next exit. They were in South Miami. "Where to?"

Stone saw a sign for a parking garage. "In there."

15

Beatrice followed the sign and made a sharp turn into a space on the third level, which was nearly deserted. "What now?"

Stone pointed the gun at her head. "We're going to get another car. Any bullshit and you will die. Try to alert anyone and you die. Understood?"

"I don't want to go with you."

"That's not how it works."

"You need to let me out."

Stone pressed the gun tight to the side of her head. "I can't do that."

She nodded, sobbing. "I don't know how this got so crazy. And I'm sorry I was part of it, but I had no idea!"

"Listen, they're going to kill you anyway."

Beatrice went quiet for a few moments, as if weighing carefully what he was saying. "Me? This has nothing to do with me."

"It does now."

"I won't say a thing."

"You still don't get it, do you? Have you ever been tortured before?"

Beatrice's face scrunched and she began to sob. "Please don't hurt me."

"I'm not talking about me. I'm talking about the guys who hired you to set me up. Don't you get it? They're going to kill you. You go to the cops, you will be dead within an hour of leaving the station."

Beatrice closed her eyes.

"You have to deal with this. You need to get yourself together. And I mean quick. This is the real world, not some make-believe shit. So you better get your ass out of this car. Now."

Beatrice nodded.

Stone cocked his head and they exited the vehicle. He scanned the garage, then gestured to a silver Audi parked a few spots away. He pulled a custom key fob out of his pocket and pointed it at the car. The device would cycle through a series of radio frequencies until it emitted a signal on the same frequency that had locked the vehicle. A couple of seconds later, he heard a hard click. The Audi door had been unlocked, also disengaging the alarm.

"Get in," he said, looking around.

Beatrice just stared at him.

"Beatrice, get in the car!"

She shook her head. "You're going to have to kill me."

Stone looked around to check that they were still alone. "I said get in the fucking car!"

She closed her eyes tight and shook her head hard, as if she were a child. "I don't want to go with you. I don't know you. I think you're going to kill me when you're through with me."

"I will let you go . . . but only when I say so. You have my word."

Beatrice shook her head.

"We either get in the car together or I kill you here. In cold blood. Do you want your daughter to lose her mommy? To grow up without you? There will be no more birthday parties."

Beatrice was breathing hard. She looked terrified.

"I'm going to count to five. And when I get to five, you will be in the car. And we'll drive out of here."

Beatrice fought back tears and began to nod.

"You'll get in the car?"

She nodded harder.

Stone opened the passenger door, and she slid in. She hunched in the seat, head in her hands.

Stone got in the driver's seat and started the car via voice activation. Then he drove out of the parking garage and back onto the road.

"Buckle up, Beatrice."

She wiped her eyes and did as she was told.

"I admire the fact you love your kid so much."

"I'm a fuck-up of a mother. What sort of mom gets involved in bullshit like this? Stuck out in the middle of goddamn Miami in the middle of the night with a psychotic lunatic."

"Things aren't great, I admit. But I won't hurt you."

"You already pointed a gun at my head. Like you were playing Russian roulette."

"You just need to come to your senses and realize what you've gotten yourself mixed up in. If they find you, you're going to wish you hadn't been born, trust me."

"Who are these guys? Is it the mafia?"

"Worse. Much worse."

Beatrice shook her head. "Much worse than the mafia? Are you kidding me?"

Stone threaded through dark roads, trying to figure out his next move. "Sadly not."

"Great. Where are we going?"

"We're going to disappear."

"We? I don't want to disappear."

Stone saw a sign he knew, took the ramp, and was back on the highway, headed southwest. "Too bad."

"What the hell does that mean?"

"It means we're going on the run for as long as we can stay alive."

Five

Kevin de Boer seethed as he sat in the front passenger seat of the car after being pulled over by cops on a Miami highway. The operation couldn't have gone worse. In the back were two South African operatives, with the American driver, ex–Navy SEAL Steve Travers, up front. No one said a word. They didn't have to.

De Boer sensed their simmering anger at the sequence of events.

They were supposed to have followed Stone to a warehouse in Miami and neutralized him, but Stone had turned the tables on them.

The cop approached the vehicle, and the driver rolled down the window.

"Can I help you, Officer?" de Boer said.

The cop shone the flashlight in his face. "Need to see your IDs, gentlemen."

De Boer handed over their false South African IDs. He ran his hands across his face, feeling the old scar on his left cheek.

The cop checked the last of the IDs before handing them back to de Boer. "So, you guys are a long way from home."

De Boer forced a smile. "Absolutely, Officer. Still a bit jet-lagged."

"What are you in Florida for?"

"It's a reunion of old friends."

The cop nodded. "Old friends, huh? Where you off to?"

"Headed down to the Keys for some fishing."

The cop shone the flashlight on the two South African operatives, then back on de Boer. "Where's your fishing gear? In the trunk?"

"No, sir. We're going to hire our equipment. Is that all, Officer?"

"Not so fast. We got a call saying that this vehicle was pursuing a woman, said it was her ex-husband. What have you got to say about that?"

De Boer looked shocked. "That's very strange, Officer. We just got off a long flight. I can only imagine she was mistaken."

"Can I see your tickets?"

De Boer rifled in his pocket and pulled out the fake airline tickets, part of their cover story.

The cop shone his flashlight on the tickets. "She was quite specific. License plate. The car make. Very specific."

"I'm at a loss to understand that, Officer."

The cop stared at him dead-eyed. He handed back the tickets. "South Africa, huh? Whereabouts?"

"Little place outside Pretoria. We're farmers. Hardworking farmers."

"Where's your luggage?"

"That was sent on down to our destination in Key West."

"You mind if I look in the trunk?"

"Go right ahead, sir."

The cop opened up the trunk, which contained a car maintenance kit. "Yeah, that's fine." He slammed the trunk shut and ambled back to the passenger-side window.

"Anything else, Officer?" de Boer said.

"I want to see your passports."

De Boer handed the cop a plastic ziplock bag with the fake passports of all three men from South Africa.

"Stay in the vehicle while I see that this all checks out."

"Very good, sir," de Boer said.

The cop went back to his car. De Boer and the other three opera-tives sat in silence. He was glad that the weapons were currently stored in a secret compartment underneath the rear seats.

De Boer took out his cell phone and called Brigadier George Reynolds, who was leading the operation. He passed on news of what was happening.

Reynolds said, "Your IDs will withstand scrutiny. As far as the cops are concerned, you're just some white South African guys on holiday in Florida. It's a good story."

De Boer shook his head. "It's a mess."

"It was the plan that made the most sense given the intel we had. Our source in the Miami police let us know that Stone was in town. We know he's here once a month and that he always visits that bar. We put the woman in place."

"But no one listened to my earlier concerns. You're still not listening."

"Kevin," Reynolds said, "you were the only one who thought we should drug him and carry him out."

"The actress, who by the way was fantastic, should have dosed his drink. Instead of spiking him, we spooked him. The audio from her phone indicated that he asked her about some fucking deli she had no clue about. If you're going to go the honey trap route, you need to prep your bait better."

"I think we've got to appreciate," Reynolds said, "that Nathan Stone is no ordinary individual."

"No kidding. We can both agree on that. The guy is a real piece of work."

"This isn't helping," Reynolds said. "It's not moving us forward."

"Got to go, George, he's coming back."

De Boer ended the call. He glanced in the side mirror and saw the cop leaning against the cruiser, lights on, talking into his radio. "If we had stabbed him after he left the bar, that would have been a smart choice too. We could have just shot him. But this? It was the right move on the wrong guy."

The driver nodded.

De Boer took a few moments to contemplate the chain of events. He began to wonder where his brother was. Time was dragging. And Stone was getting farther away. He turned to Roel Bakker in the rear seat. "Check to see if Pieter is within range."

Bakker called de Boer's brother, Pieter, who was the mobile operative on the mission. The backup. He was on a high-powered motorbike and had been tailing Stone from a distance. "Pieter, your brother wants to speak to you."

De Boer took the cell phone. "Pieter, where are you?"

"I'm just . . ." The call from his brother's voice-activated helmet was cutting out. "Repeat . . . I have a visual . . ."

"Pieter, I repeat, have you got eyes on the target?"

"I see them. I have a visual. Coming into Homestead."

De Boer felt a surge of adrenaline. "Copy that. What else?"

"They're driving a silver Audi."

"Is the girl with him?"

"Affirmative!"

De Boer clenched his fist. "Good. How far from them?"

"Half a mile."

"Do not lose them. I repeat, do not lose them."

"Do I have authorization?"

"Affirmative. Take them both out."

Six

The GPS indicated that the car was near Homestead, in South Florida. Rural, isolated, the edge of nowhere.

"Where the hell are you taking me?" Beatrice asked.

Stone knew the area well. He'd spent the past two nights at a motel nearby. No point going there. If the Commission knew he'd be at that bar, they'd been monitoring the rest of his movements too. He headed west out of the backwater town, headlights leading the way.

"I said, where the hell are we going?"

"Try to relax."

"Please tell me where we're going. You said I could get out."

"You can. But not yet. When I say."

She unbuckled her seat belt. "I'm going to jump out here if you don't stop and let me out."

Stone accelerated to seventy. "Good luck with that. You'll be a vegetable if you jump out now. Not a surgeon in the world will be able to reconstruct your face."

Beatrice bowed her head as if defeated.

"They played you real nice. They probably ran a credit check on you and saw they had a desperate woman who would do just about anything, even if it sounded improbable. Here's the thing: if it sounds too good to be true, it probably is."

Beatrice began to sob. "What a fucking mess!"

"Tell me about it. I went out for a few beers, and now I'm being hunted by some pros no doubt hired by people you don't want to know. Trust me. And make no mistake, they will be figuring out where we are as I speak. So you need to get yourself together."

Beatrice stared at the dark road ahead of them, headlights picking out the palm trees. "Where are you taking me? I can't see any lights. There's no houses. Are you going to fucking kill me?"

Stone said nothing.

Beatrice hugged herself and bowed her head. She began to do what sounded like breathing exercises.

Stone was only interested in disappearing. Ideally by himself. But he knew that if she got out, or he let her out—at least now—the Commission would kill her.

"What do you do?" she asked him.

Stone wasn't in the mood for discussion.

"Just tell me."

"It doesn't matter."

"What do you mean, *it doesn't matter*? It does to me. At least now it does!"

"Listen, you wouldn't believe me even if I told you."

"Try me."

Stone sighed.

"So, are you going to enlighten me? What's this all about? What do you do? Who are you?"

"I kill people."

Beatrice took a few moments to contemplate that. "What?"

"I kill for a living. That's what I do."

"You're an assassin?"

"You could call it that."

Beatrice was quiet for a while before she spoke. "That's not what I wanted to hear."

"You wanted to know. Well, now you know."

Beatrice reached for the door handle, and Stone grabbed her by the arm with one hand, keeping the other on the steering wheel.

"Don't even think about it."

"I need to get out of here! I need to pee. You're hurting me."

"Don't try and open the door. You will die."

"But you're going to kill me anyway. Look, I need to pee."

Stone ignored her comments and let go of her.

Beatrice touched her arm. "What was that all about?"

"What do you think it was?"

"You grabbed me. I think you left a bruise."

"Listen, I don't want to hurt you."

"Promise?"

"I don't make promises. I give you my word."

"How do I know that I can trust you?"

"You don't."

Beatrice sat in silence.

Stone drove on through the dark.

"This is literally in the middle of nowhere."

"Probably."

"Tell me why they want to kill you. Tell me who exactly wants you dead. I need to know what the fuck this is all about."

Stone sighed again.

"I'm waiting."

"It's not the sort of thing you really want to know."

"Try me."

"I was hired by an organization a couple of years back to kill a guy."

Beatrice buried her face in her hands. "You're not joking, are you?"

"No, I'm not."

"So, did you kill this guy? Who was he?"

"You don't need to know. The operation was overseas. But it all went to shit. I destroyed a facility owned by the people who hired me."

"Shit."

"Then they kidnapped my sister."

"Why?"

"Why what?"

"Why did they kidnap your sister?"

Stone shrugged. "Payback."

"You're shitting me?"

Stone stared straight ahead and drove.

"Are you kidding me? Is that what this is?"

"It's the truth. So now you know."

"Jimmy, this sounds . . . So, they want to kill you now for what exactly?"

"I managed to turn the tables on the whole organization. Wiped them out. Or so I thought."

"Now they've found out where you are and used me to . . . what exactly?"

"Lure me to an imaginary party, where no doubt I would have been killed, you too."

Beatrice shook her head. "This is certifiable. I don't like hearing stuff like this."

"Now you know what you're dealing with. Trust me, these people— you don't want them to get you."

"These people . . ." She shivered.

"You've got a choice. You either take your chances with the guys who are after me. Or you learn to trust me."

"Trust you? Why the fuck should I trust you?"

"Your choice."

"Some fucking choice. Christ, what about my family?"

Stone checked the GPS.

"Where are you taking me?"

"If I wanted to kill you, I would've killed you by now. So I'd appreciate if you could just focus on the fact that we are both going to die if they get their hands on us."

Beatrice sighed. "I fucking need to pee. Where are we now?"

"Main Park Road. Headed southwest, if you must know."

"No idea where that is."

"Yeah."

"I can't see anything. It's pitch black. Just the asphalt. And the grass. And some trees."

"Do you honestly not know where you are?"

"Somewhere in Florida?"

Stone didn't tell her that they were now approaching the River of Grass. One of the great American wildernesses. The Everglades.

Seven

A musty aroma from the nearby mangrove swamps seeped through the car's vents. Stone stared at the dark road. His mind flashed back to the last time he'd been here, ten years before. He remembered being dragged from the grassy shallows, slipping into unconsciousness, close to death. Lungs filled with brackish water. He remembered harsh chopper lights in the darkness. Faces staring down at him. Everything slowed.

He'd wanted to speak but he couldn't. Couldn't breathe either. He'd realized he was close to checking out of this world. Then all was darkness.

The next thing he remembered was waking up in a hospital in Saudi Arabia, his handler having smuggled him out of the country in the dead of night. It had been a botched assassination attempt. Before long there was a death announcement. Fake death certificate. Nathan Stone had died. At least officially. A funeral was mocked up. He hadn't known it at the time. But it had all been part of a plan to resurrect him with a new face, new look, new name. He'd been transferred to the Commission's facility in Scotland, where he was kept in isolation while they monitored his recovery. Eventually, he was ready to be deployed again. The new assassin. Primed to kill.

All these thoughts swam around his head as he drove on in silence.

Stone knew their current predicament was dire. The reality was they would be lucky to still be alive in twenty-four hours. The Commission had come for him. Nathan going on the run with the woman they'd hired wouldn't dissuade them. If anything, it would enrage them. Then make them focus. Nathan tried to imagine how they would react. He thought he and Beatrice might have a few hours' head start. But the Commission would deploy a team, and that team would find them. Of that he had no doubt.

Surveillance technology today was so pervasive, the Commission could find them anywhere. What they needed to do was drop off the grid completely. Disappear. And the Everglades was the best place he knew of to do that. A raw wilderness. Untamed.

Stone wondered who was calling the shots on this operation. He thought he'd brought down the whole organization when he killed Clayton Wilson and all the others in New York. But it was clear the entity was still alive. He assumed Berenger, the Commission's in-house shrink—the guy who'd signed off on Stone's fitness for his first mission after his resurrection—was still around. He'd always been there, moving in the shadows, organizing. Planning.

The soft-spoken psychologist. Berenger was, like Stone—like most of those associated with the Commission—former CIA. And that was the other possibility that presented itself: that this private offshoot of the CIA was no longer entirely off the books, in the shadows. Was this attempt to take him out being run out of Langley?

The more Nathan thought about his predicament, the gloomier he felt. What a fucking mess. It was possible they were already closing in and he just didn't know it.

Stone was also angry with himself for taking the risk of heading to Miami for a few days of R & R. How could he have been so undisciplined thinking that his reconfigured face wouldn't ping up among all the cameras in a big American city? In South Beach, cameras were everywhere. Bars, restaurants, all over.

Had he gotten careless, making such bad judgments? Was it bad luck? He wondered why he hadn't been more alert. He had stayed down and around the Keys for the most part but also spent some time in a crummy motel room, where he could monitor his sister.

He knew better than anyone that big cities were a magnet for surveillance cameras. Then he began to wonder if, subconsciously perhaps, he wanted to be caught. Wanted it to be over. Was that it?

Beatrice turned and glared at him. "Do you know this area?" she asked.

"Yeah. I know it well enough."

"So, do you kill people out here?" When he didn't answer, she said, "Great. So, are you going to tell me?"

"Tell you what?"

"Where you're taking me." Beatrice unbuckled her seat belt and reached for the door.

Stone braked hard and brought the car to a grinding halt. He grabbed her by the arm again. "Don't be so stupid."

"I need to pee."

Stone shook his head. "Fine. Pee. And then we go."

Beatrice got out of the car. Before he knew it, she was sprinting back down the dark road they had just traveled.

"Are you fucking kidding me?" Stone jumped out of the car and pursued the rapidly retreating figure, who was screaming like a banshee. "Get back here!" he roared.

Beatrice was running hard despite her high heels.

The drone of a distant engine pierced the humid night air. It seemed to be getting closer. Then a speck of light appeared out of the darkness. Farther down the dark road. A mile or so away. A lone biker came into sight.

Beatrice ran, waving her arms. "Help! Stop!"

Stone immediately realized the potential danger. But he couldn't be sure. He pulled the Glock out of his waistband. He took aim as the bike roared toward Beatrice. "Get out of the way!" he shouted to her.

Beatrice kept on running wildly. The road was bathed in a ghostly glow from the moon above and the bike speeding toward them. The scene played out as if in slow motion.

Stone saw the biker reach down to a leg strap. He was sure there was a gun. But he didn't wait to find out.

He squeezed the trigger twice.

The shots rang out in the sultry night. Birds screeched as they flew out of their nests in the trees.

The biker went over as he lost control. The sound of metal scraping as he tumbled across the road, sliding with the bike into a ditch. The smell of burning rubber.

Beatrice turned and screamed.

Stone ran over to the ditch. The guy was lying beside the mangled bike. Twisted hand still gripping the gun, smeared in mud and grass. Stone yanked the gun from the man's hand and threw it away into the long grass. He ripped off the biker's visor. The guy's eyes were glassy and open, blood spilling out of his mouth. He tried to speak.

Stone pressed his gun to the guy's forehead. He stared down.

The guy blinked.

Stone could hear only his strained breathing. He needed to know if there were others. Were they on their way? He could see the guy was close to death.

He put his gun back into his waistband. Then he dragged the guy through the trees that fringed the road and into the marshy grasses. Squelching through the muddy ground. He rifled in the guy's pockets and found a cell phone, which he slid into his pocket.

Stone retrieved the bike from the ditch. Then he maneuvered it through the twisted hardwood and cypress trees to the same spot as the biker's body, hidden in the deep grass. Both out of sight from the road.

Stone was panting as he pushed his way back through the lush vegetation. Long grass, trees, then back on the dark road. He turned and saw that Beatrice was now a few hundred yards away. He sprinted after her. He was still pretty far away from her. But when she glanced back, she stumbled, and that gave Stone the advantage he needed.

A few seconds later and he had caught up with her.

"What the fuck do you think you're doing?" he asked, grabbing her arm.

"Go to hell!"

Stone dragged her back down the road; she cursed at him the whole time. He was lucky there were no passing cars. This was getting seriously out of hand. His mind was made up. The Everglades were their only option now. And he needed to get them there quick. He dropped the biker's cell phone down a storm drain so they couldn't track it on GPS. Then he strapped her back into her seat.

Beatrice looked exhausted, her face flushed.

"Not smart," he said.

"Why did you kill him!"

"I shot him. I didn't kill him."

"You shot him? Why?"

"He was one of them. He was going to kill us."

"One of them. What does that mean?"

"It means we need to get out of here."

"I hate you! I fucking hate you!" She clawed at his face.

Stone grabbed her hands to restrain her. "Haven't you been listening to what I've been saying? I'm trying to put space between us and them. Now, if you're so dumb that you don't mind being caught by these people, then that's your choice. But it's not mine. I have dealt with these people, and they do not reason. What they do is kill. Ask questions later. And that's if you're lucky."

Beatrice wailed, "Is he dead?"

"He will be soon."

"I want to go home! I want out of here! You said I could go!"

"Not while you're jeopardizing my life."

"What?"

"Anything that stops me from getting away from them is putting me at a disadvantage. My sister has no one but me looking out for her. If they manage to kill me, they'll either kill her too or leave her to rot. I'm not going to allow that to happen. And I will not allow any two-bit actress to get in my way." Stone released his grip. "Do you understand?"

Beatrice sobbed hard and took off her seat belt. "Please let me go."

Stone slid back into the driver's seat, slamming his door shut. He hit the gas and accelerated hard. "Buckle up."

She sighed and did as she was told.

"Now, I said I was going to let you go. And I was. But you're causing me problems, and I can't have that. The easy solution would be to kill you here and now. Do you understand and appreciate that fact?"

Beatrice nodded.

"Good. Now we're getting somewhere. Do you see anyone else on this road?"

"No."

"That's right. There is no one here. And I have not killed you."

"You shot him . . . I can't believe you shot him."

"It had to be done."

"You're going to kill me. I know it."

"I'm not going to kill you. But I can assure you that guy's crew will be trying to pick up our trail one way or the other. They will find us if you act like that—running off, calling attention to us. Keep doing that and there's a distinct possibility that they will find us before you even get to talk to the cops."

They drove in silence along the deserted road for a few more miles. Stone checked the GPS. His mind was racing as he considered his options. Beatrice was clearly going to be a problem if he kept her with him. But if he wanted to keep her alive, that meant dragging her along.

He stopped the car in the middle of the road. He switched off the headlights. "Get out," he said.

Beatrice got out and stood, arms folded, beside the darkened road.

Stone maneuvered the car through the shoulder-high trees and grass lining the road. He shut off the engine and got out. Satisfied the Audi was out of sight, Stone looked at Beatrice. "I've got a plan."

"What does that mean?"

"It means we're headed where no one can find us. At least for a while, until I figure this out."

"You're starting to sound paranoid."

"Maybe I am."

"This is getting seriously nuts. I want to get back to my life."

"So do I. But we need to be smart."

Beatrice sighed. "So why don't we just leave Florida now?"

Stone grabbed her by the arm and hauled her along the dark road, the pale gleam of the moon bathing the asphalt, illuminating the way.

"I don't want to go." She tried to break free from his grip.

Stone held on to her.

Beatrice struggled free. "Don't fucking touch me."

Stone grabbed her arm again. "How many times do I have to tell you?" he said, marching her along the road. "You need to move! There will be others who will come after us."

Beatrice began to sob again. "I can't fucking believe this. Get your hands off me!"

Stone spotted a small dirt trail leading into the darkness, shrouded by cypress trees and grass and foliage. A trail he'd hiked many times.

Stone pulled Beatrice down the dirt trail. A few moments later she broke free and began to run again. He ran after her and launched himself at her, knocking her to the ground.

Stone maneuvered her onto her back and sat astride her as she tried to claw and bite him. He held her wrists tight and pinned them to the earth.

She spat up at him. "Fuck you! Let me go, you sick fuck!"

Stone felt a surge of anger rise to the surface. An anger that he sometimes managed to keep in check. But she was pressing all his buttons.

"I said let me go!" She spat again.

Stone wiped the spittle off his face. He hauled her to her feet and pointed the Glock at her head. "You've got a choice now. You either head down the trail or I will shoot you dead. Here and now. Makes no difference to me."

Beatrice was nearly hysterical, sobbing and screaming.

"No one will hear you. So you need to focus."

"I don't want to focus, you bastard."

Stone pulled back the slide. "Last chance. Answer me or you die! Here and now!"

"I want to live! Please, I want to live!"

"So do I. So we walk."

Beatrice hung her head low as if resigned to her fate.

"You do what you're told, and you will live. I can't have you fucking flagging down some motorist first thing in the morning. You can guarantee they will be swarming that road at first light. They're closing in. So, what's it going to be?"

"Please don't hurt me. I'm not good with pain. Can't you see I'm scared?"

Stone pressed the gun tight to her head.

"Okay, I'll walk." She wiped the tears from her face as she followed him back down the trail. "So, where are we walking to?"

"You'll see."

"Christ, there is nothing here. I'm in the middle of fucking nowhere."

"We're on the edge of nowhere. You're dawdling. Walk in front of me."

Stone waited for her to catch up and followed a few yards behind her.

She swatted some bugs. "The fuck is this?"

"It's southern Florida. Deal with it."

She smiled with imitation sweetness. "Are you going to shoot me in the head, tough guy?"

"If you don't shut up, that can be arranged."

"Un-fucking-believable. What is it with men and the wilderness?"

"What do you know about men?"

"A lot, trust me. And you're all a bunch of bastards."

Stone shook his head, sweat beading his forehead. His shirt was sticking to his back. The smell of the ancient mangroves and the brackish water wafted in the sticky air.

"You going to rape me out here? Well, I'd rather you shoot me in the back of the fucking head, you scumbag."

Stone ignored her. They walked on in silence for a few minutes. The bugs were biting like crazy. Beatrice was shaking out her hair and swatting everything she could.

"That'll be just great. I get kidnapped and then end up dying of fucking malaria or Zika or some shit."

"You've got some mouth on you."

"Fuck you."

"Nice."

Beatrice began to slow down until she stopped, hands on hips.

Stone pushed her forward down the trail.

"Hey, do you mind?" she said.

"Keep moving until we get to the water."

"The water? What water?"

"This is the River of Grass."

"You decided to drown me, is that it?"

"Keep walking."

"Where exactly are we, so I can tell the cops?"

Stone knew the area well. It was the Snake Bight Trail. He wanted to get out of there before they bumped into early-morning hikers. Animal noises sounded in the distance, and he could hear night birds rustling in flight.

He used the back of his arm to wipe the sweat from his brow.

And they walked. Deeper and deeper into the Everglades. Away from civilization. Away from *them*.

Eight

It was the dead of night when a Gulfstream, registered to a company in the Caymans, landed on the prairie airstrip in Wyoming. Armed guards confiscated Dr. Mark Berenger's cell phone as he walked down the steps. He was scanned for any surveillance equipment. Satisfied that there were no listening devices on him, the men drove Berenger in an SUV to a huge house on a nearby ranch.

A butler wearing white gloves showed him into a dimly lit dining room.

Berenger was left alone with his thoughts for a few minutes until the butler returned, serving him coffee.

"He'll be with you very soon," the butler said. "Please make yourself comfortable."

Berenger had never visited this property. He had only met the man he knew as Fisk once. Truth be told, he was rather apprehensive about this second meeting. Berenger was carrying the mantle as the head of the newly configured Commission, which meant that Fisk's approval or disapproval landed entirely on him.

The more he thought about their current mission—not going as smoothly as he'd like—the more he wondered how much blood it would take to bring down Stone. More than Stone had already spilled trying to destroy the Commission?

Berenger wasn't surprised Stone was proving so elusive. So dangerous. He knew better than anyone what made Nathan Stone tick. That was why he had been picked to lead the remnants of the shadowy group. The ghosts of those who had perished at Stone's hands lingered in his mind, transforming his usually analytical thoughts into seething anger. Where previously he had obsessed about Stone's psychological makeup, now he wondered only what it would take to bring him down. He had, unbeknownst to anyone, visited Stone's childhood home. He had tried to absorb the environment. He kept grainy photographs in his study at home of Stone as a boy, with his mother. He'd studied the emptiness and sadness in Stone's eyes. The mother's proud features. Berenger had also read up on Stone's violent alcoholic father. His influence pervaded everything in Stone's life. Like a ghost from his past who was forever with him.

Stone had a remarkable psychological makeup, and it made him a truly terrifying figure. It was as if Stone could sense a man's fear up close. His vulnerabilities. He had an almost animalistic ability to sense danger.

Berenger was out of the loop in many ways. He had not been part of the inner circle during the previous operation, which had ended in such terrible failure. He had watched in grim fascination as Stone had wreaked his terrible revenge. Destroyed facilities. Destroyed lives.

The reason Berenger had been invited to the ranch today was because of Stone. The mission to kill him had run into trouble. And he was here to either explain why or perhaps outline the next move to kill Stone. The buck stopped with Berenger. And that made him nervous.

His instincts told him that the man he was about to speak with could have him deleted, and no one would be the wiser. He could be disappeared as and when Fisk saw fit for any perception of failure or for no reason at all.

Berenger pondered that for a few moments. He wondered if he should have accepted the post when he was offered it. Was it just vanity that had led him to think his medical knowledge qualified him for this role? Pride? Delusions of grandeur? Narcissism?

Berenger drank his coffee and sighed. He missed not having his phone. He wanted to make sure his wife was okay. But as it stood, his main concern was the ongoing operation to find Nathan Stone.

The door opened behind him. Berenger turned at the sound.

The butler smiled. "He'll see you now in the library."

Berenger followed the butler down a long corridor, which led down stairs and through security doors, before he was ushered into the carpeted library.

Fisk was sitting in an armchair staring out at the staggering vista, the Rocky Mountains silhouetted in the distance. "Take a seat beside me, Mark."

Berenger did as he was told.

"I don't sleep too much these days."

"If you're in need of a prescription . . ."

Fisk waved off the suggestion. "Hope your flight up from Florida was okay."

"Bit of turbulence over Arkansas. Nothing to write home about."

Fisk gazed out through the glass at the breathtaking view. "This is what we fight for. To be free. To wake up each and every day in a free country."

"Indeed."

"I love this country, Mark. I know you do too. It needs men like us to deal with unsavory things. And yes, by that I mean neutralizing an American senator, journalist, or whatever it takes. We have an agenda. And we thought Nathan Stone was the man to carry it out. We invested so much in him over the years—the reconstructive surgery, the medical bills, keeping his goddamn sister in that nice hospital. We picked up everything, but he went bad on us, Mark."

"I know that only too well, sir."

"He went rogue twice. And he wiped out the previous group. Good friends the lot of them."

"I know, sir."

"Patriots. Fierce patriots. And our work to delete the Canadian prime minister was very nearly compromised. But we got lucky in the end on that one."

Berenger sighed. "Stone will be neutralized, sir."

"Our organization can't move on with its work while he's alive. He knows too much. And I fear it's just a matter of time before he's picked up by the Feds. God knows where that will end."

"We'll find him. And he will be taken care of, believe me."

"I've got a bad feeling about this already. Surely, in God's name, it isn't difficult to kill one man. This is America, after all."

Berenger cleared his throat. "Sir, first, I take full responsibility for what's happened. I appointed Brigadier Reynolds as operations chief. So any blame lies solely with me."

"Reynolds is a good man. But the others I've spoken to on the team say he made the wrong call on the approach to Stone."

"Sir, I'm offering my resignation with immediate effect. I'm a man of honor, and I have and will take absolute responsibility."

Fisk stared off into the distance as if contemplating his next move. "He's an interesting character this Nathan Stone."

"Indeed."

"He takes down the entire facility in Scotland . . . then destroys everyone in the Commission. By himself! It defies belief."

Berenger sighed as he shifted in his seat.

"Now we seem to have let him slip through our hands again. Reynolds should have handled this better. Dazzling career. Special operations. CIA. He's been there, done that. And he knows the drill."

Berenger felt his stomach tighten. "I thought the honey trap was a terrific idea."

"Why did you pick that particular actress?"

"She was deep in debt. She was desperate. But also she bore a striking resemblance to Stone's sister. I figured this aspect, knowing what I know about Stone, would confuse his judgment, reassure him too."

"Don't get me wrong, it was a terrific idea," Fisk said. "But I'm running this through my head. I know about these things too. Shouldn't she have lured him outside, where he could have been taken care of? There's a goddamn alley down the side of the bar, just off Fourteenth Street."

"Hindsight is a wonderful thing."

"She could have drugged him, jabbed him with some Fentanyl, a million ways to do it. He is now on the loose. Am I right?"

Berenger sighed. "To be more accurate, he's on the loose with the actress we hired."

"Against her will?"

"We don't know."

Fisk pinched the bridge of his nose. "What's the latest?"

"Just before my plane landed, sir, I checked in. We have three teams working on this around the clock. They're scouring a location near Homestead, in Florida. The last known location of one of the operatives. Pieter de Boer. But I think on reflection it was handled incorrectly. The setup to bait him was wrong. Reynolds—"

"Reynolds is out."

Berenger felt his throat tighten. "Sir, I am one hundred percent responsible for appointing Reynolds."

"You stay. You know the inner workings of Stone's head better than anyone. You understand the target on a psychological level. I like that. But with regards to Reynolds, he's gone. Am I clear?"

Berenger nodded. "Very, sir."

"I want you to see this through. You're still growing into the position, Mark, I understand that. But if you feel things are not going according to plan, my rule of thumb is always to change the plan."

"I hear what you're saying."

"This is not a criticism of you. The blame lies squarely with the military man who had that responsibility."

Berenger took a few moments to consider his reply. "Who takes over the operational planning from Reynolds?"

"Tell me your thoughts on Kevin de Boer," Fisk said. "I like how he talks. I like how forthright he is. I've spoken to some experts within South African intelligence too. But I'm keen to hear your observations."

"He's very impressive. And as you say, he speaks his mind. The fact that he instructed his brother to join the revised mission shows strong leadership."

"Pieter de Boer is dead."

"We don't know that for sure," Berenger said.

"I believe Kevin raised concerns with Reynolds from the outset about the honey trap."

Berenger cleared his throat. "Absolutely correct. He did voice concerns about how we were going to execute the trap. To be fair, his voice was the only objection."

"Exactly." Fisk ran his hands through his hair. "In my eyes, what has transpired lends credence to Kevin de Boer's instincts."

Berenger nodded. "The fact that de Boer foresaw a problem when no one else did shows brilliant critical-thinking skills. I should have opened up the strategy to more scrutiny. I made the call, and it was the wrong one."

"Don't beat yourself up, Mark. The question is, What do you want to do now?"

"I want to find and neutralize Nathan Stone—and the girl—without further delay."

Fisk smiled. "So, how would you feel about Kevin de Boer taking over as director of operations? Reporting to you. And you alone."

"Very good," Berenger said.

Fisk steepled his fingers, deep in thought. "Where do you think Stone is headed?"

"I think the Everglades looks like a smart choice."

"How do we pick up the scent again?"

"I have a plan to boost our cyberteam with immediate effect. We need far better technical data. Real-time feeds."

"Whatever it takes. We need to find Stone. And end this once and for all."

"What about the girl?" Berenger asked.

"The girl knows too much. Eliminate her."

Berenger felt himself begin to smile.

Nine

Beatrice was walking down the dark trail at the edge of the Everglades, Stone close behind. The full moon lent enough light that they were making good time, but he was all too aware of how soon dawn would arrive and leave them more exposed. Suddenly, he saw something move on the trail in front of Beatrice.

"Freeze!" Stone said.

Beatrice stopped.

"Not another step forward. Stay perfectly still."

She turned to look at him. "What is it?"

Stone took a few steps forward and aimed at the ground. Two shots rang out. They tore into the oily black skin of a cottonmouth snake.

Beatrice shrieked in horror. "What the hell?"

The moonlight illuminated the writhing snake. A few moments later it stopped moving.

Stone waited a bit before he stepped forward and kicked the dead snake into the bushes at the side of the dirt trail. "It's okay, relax."

"Damn." She looked at him, fear in her eyes. "I don't like it here."

"Keep going."

Beatrice shook her head as she swatted the mosquitos biting her arms. "I just want to go back."

"Don't you understand what I've been telling you? You need to reset your life from here on. What's in the past is in the past. Your old life is gone."

"No, it's not."

"Yes, it is. The biker was just the opening salvo, trust me. You just don't realize it yet. But you will. Trust me."

"I'm not an outdoor person. This is hell for me."

"I get that. But you really need to keep moving. Because when the sun comes up, they'll be casting their net for us."

"I can't believe this is happening."

Stone grabbed her by the arms and shook her. "Let's go!"

She turned and stomped down the trail.

Stone followed in her wake. Up ahead, glistening dark waters lapped the shore. He saw the outline of a small boat tied up with a rope near a wooden boardwalk.

The type of boat used by Everglades rangers.

Stone prodded Beatrice forward. "In the boat!"

She turned, her eyes glassy from crying. "I can't."

"Listen, you want to walk all the way back along the trail again? Do you? If there was one cottonmouth, there will be dozens more."

Beatrice started hyperventilating and rubbing her face hard with the palms of her hands. "Have you got any Xanax?"

Stone burst out laughing, the unexpected sound startling birds into flight, silhouetted against the pale moon. "Do I look like the sort of guy that carries around Xanax? No, I don't."

"I suffer from multiple ailments."

"No kidding."

Beatrice squatted down for a few moments, as if exhausted and traumatized by it all.

"Get up!"

She groaned as she stood up straight. "I want to die. I would rather die than live like this. I can't cope with this."

"Get in the boat."

"Or what?"

"Just get in. And we can discuss how I plan to get us out of here."

"You're the one who got us in here! In the middle of fucking nowhere! On a goddamn trail that leads to the water. I can't see a thing. I want to go home!"

Stone grabbed her by the shoulders. "You're still alive. If I wanted to kill you, I could've done that when I killed that goddamn biker."

Beatrice grew quiet, brushing some bugs out of her hair.

"You're alive. Don't you get it? If you try and disappear from *them*, you are as good as dead. With me? You have a chance."

"So you're my protector now, huh? Lucky me!"

"I'm your only fucking chance!"

Beatrice turned and looked back down the trail. Then she looked at the dark waters up ahead. "What's out there?"

"What do you think?"

"I'm asking you a goddamn straightforward question."

"This is the Everglades. Tropical wetlands. Mangrove swamps. Hundreds of tiny islands. It's a tough place to survive. But it's a good place to hide out. For now."

Beatrice bowed her head before she turned to face him. "Jimmy, I'm scared."

Stone sighed. "Listen, we've wasted enough time. You either retrace our steps, or you get in the boat. Your choice. I'm done with this discussion."

Beatrice hung her head low. "You say they'll kill me . . . How can you be so sure?"

"Head back that way and you'll find out yourself. Do you think the biker just wanted to make friends?"

Beatrice looked down the dark trail again, then stared back out over the black water. She sighed. "I'm not going to make it, am I?"

"You can do this. I promise. But it's not going to be easy. I'll try and help you."

"But I can go if I want?"

"You're free to go."

Beatrice looked at him, her face bathed in moonlight. "My instincts are saying you're dangerous and I'd be nuts to get in the boat."

Stone said nothing.

"But a tiny voice inside me is also telling me that you could have killed me and you haven't. Better the devil you know maybe."

Stone looked out over the water. "We don't know what's out there. But you sure as hell *do* know what's waiting for you if you turn around. They will kill you. I had to take that guy out or we would both be dead."

"So, where are you going in the boat?"

"There are tiny islands all throughout the Everglades. I plan on getting to one and hunkering down."

"For how long?"

"As long as it takes."

"No guarantees?"

"No guarantees."

She shook her head, climbed into the small boat, and made her way to the bow. "I must be mad. I must be absolutely fucking insane."

Stone tried hard not to smile. "You might want to face the direction we're going to be traveling."

Beatrice turned herself around. She muttered to herself.

Stone leaned over and untied the rope, which was attached to a wooden stake in the ground. Then he pushed off and climbed into the boat. He lifted one of the two oars and began to paddle out of the inland shallows and through the mangrove waters. There were bugs everywhere. Mosquitos bit their sweaty arms and necks.

"Goddamn!" Beatrice shrieked, swatting something away from her face.

"You need to think of these things in a different way."

"Oh yeah, what sort of way is that?"

"These are minor inconveniences. Annoying. Learn to roll with it."

"It's dark, I'm in a boat with some crazy guy who just shot someone—a guy who is holding me at gunpoint in the middle of the Everglades—and you tell me to learn to roll with it? Are you serious?"

Stone didn't answer. In the moon's glow he saw the eyes of an alligator that was resting on a small islet twenty yards away. Nathan steered away from land and out into the water. Ibises, egrets, and herons swooped low as the boat went past.

His mind was racing as he considered the options in front of him. There were no great options, that was the truth. It was just a matter of gambling on the least worst one. He knew that at first light things could change. *They* might very well find the motorbike, the dead guy, and the car, then head down the trail.

Stone had to assume that his pursuers would redouble their efforts. He had a head start. But it wouldn't last. The Commission wasn't done with him. Not by a long shot. They hadn't even gotten started.

Ten

Just before dawn, Catherine Hudson was pacing the deserted office in downtown Arlington, occasionally glancing at the real-time video feeds of the operatives in a Sarasota meeting room, sound turned down. She couldn't believe this was turning into such a debacle. When her cell phone rang, she expected it to be her irate boss. Instead the caller ID said it was her husband.

"Honey," he said, "you said you'd be home by two. It's now past four. What the hell happened?"

Hudson's heart sank. She took a moment to compose herself. "John, I'm sorry."

"Sorry?"

"I know it's not ideal."

"Do you know what time it is?"

"I told you, the client is super-demanding, and I'm having to rework our figures."

"What?"

"There are three other consulting firms pitching them. And I have to make sure that we win this account."

"It's four in the goddamn morning! Are you nuts? Honey, I have to be up in one and a half hours, but I'm worrying about where you are. Kirsty was crying earlier."

Hudson closed her eyes. She knew her eight-year-old daughter missed her and struggled to sleep when she wasn't in the house. "Please don't throw that guilt trip on me, John. That's so unfair."

"It's always about you, isn't it?"

"Kirsty will be fine. I know what she's like."

"Do you?"

"Oh come on, John, give me a break."

"We need to talk about this, Catherine. The nanny is out sick, and I can't take any more time off work. My job is vital to this family."

"As is mine! John, you're not the only one up to your neck in work. I'm busting my butt to get these figures ready, I'm working around the clock, and I need you to be more supportive."

He sighed. "I'm worried for you, Catherine. I'm worried for us. This can't go on."

"John, I'm really busy."

"Are you kidding me? At four in the morning? Do you take me for an idiot?"

"What is that supposed to mean?"

"I don't believe you have to work at this time of night. It's ridiculous."

"John, I need to go. I've got a report to finish."

"Go to hell."

The line went dead.

Hudson felt a sadness wash over her. She was deflated. She sensed she was losing her husband. A man she truly loved. A good man. A hardworking family man. A clever man who was no fool.

She sat down behind her desk, trying to push her domestic woes to one side. She felt bad about the web of lies she had to use to conceal what she was really doing. No one in her family knew what she did. That was not an option.

Her family believed she was a management consultant who advised companies on restructurings and cost savings. They believed that she traveled around the world, visiting clients, advising them on how to better manage their companies. It was a cover story she had put in place when she left Colby College top of her class, majoring in economics. She had been recruited by the CIA before she even graduated.

She loved her family, but they didn't need to know what she did. Her trips overseas were invariably to Afghanistan, Iraq, or Turkey. But her narrative was that she was visiting clients in the Middle East. Sometimes the Far East.

The last five years, Hudson had worked predominantly in and around DC. Mostly satellite offices in McLean and Arlington. She liked to move around. But only she knew exactly what was happening with the shadowy organization she had assembled—the Commission.

Hudson's strategy was one she'd pitched to her boss deep in the bowels of CIA HQ. He had listened to the rationale that the Agency outsourcing the assassinations of troublesome politicians and individuals would enable plausible deniability. The Commission was set up to be self-contained. She didn't have any day-to-day control over or communication with the group. They pursued carefully agreed-upon goals, and they were free to implement strategic "accidents" of influential politicians, businesspeople, and journalists as they saw fit. She was responsible, but she wasn't pulling the strings.

But recently Hudson had begun to worry about the future of the organization. She was increasingly concerned that the "ghost" operative, Nathan Stone, had still not been taken out, as had been agreed. And it followed two earlier examples of Stone going rogue, nearly bringing down the entire Commission.

She had become concerned that their financial backer, John Fisk Jr., a billionaire recluse, had made a terrible error by trying to rebuild the Commission by putting the organization's ex-CIA psychologist in charge. So far it had backfired spectacularly.

She needed to get a grip on the situation before it got any more out of hand. But that was easier said than done, especially as she'd ceded day-to-day control of the Commission.

Boxed in by her own rules, she had endured numerous sleepless nights and sent countless emails to her boss requesting that the protocols governing the operations of the Commission be updated.

She wondered why she hadn't heard back.

The main sticking point might be Fisk and how he would react to being ousted. Was that a consideration? A powerful billionaire with friends across the intelligence community and the world of politics wasn't the type to be trifled with. What if Fisk didn't go quietly? What then? Then there was the rather delicate matter of her family connections to Fisk. A man she had known since she was a little girl.

The more she thought of it, the more she realized that taking back control from the Commission was not going to be without some bad feelings. She understood that any reorganization would have to be dealt with very carefully. But despite everything that had transpired, Hudson was still in the dark as to the future of the Commission.

Hudson stared at the real-time feed from the car containing the four operatives, including the new operations director, Kevin de Boer, a highly capable operative she had known for years, having used the former special forces soldier and his team in covert operations in Lesotho and Zimbabwe.

But the news that Nathan Stone, of all people, had evaded their honey trap and was now on the run in South Florida, with a member of the public, an actress, meant she couldn't ignore the fallout any longer. She knew she was breaking the cardinal rule she had instituted from the outset. She had vowed never to be in direct contact with members of the Commission while it was "live."

Hudson's cell phone rang, snapping her out of her thoughts. She expected it to be her husband again, wondering if she was on her way home yet. But she didn't recognize the number on the caller ID.

"Catherine, is this line secure?" It was her boss, Director of the National Clandestine Service William Black.

"Yes, sir."

"I just got your message that you wanted to talk. At this time of night?"

"I'm sorry, sir, but we've got a problem."

"Couldn't it have waited till morning?"

"Sorry, sir, no, it couldn't."

A long sigh. "Give me a few moments. I'm going to transfer the call to my study. Hang on."

Hudson listened to Bach playing quietly as she hung on the line. Her stomach began to tighten with the tension.

"There, that's better," Black said. "Okay, I'm now out of earshot. So what's the goddamn urgency?"

Hudson leaned back in her seat as she stared at the feed coming out of Florida. She quickly outlined for Black the botched attempt to snare Stone and his escape with the actress.

"Are you fucking kidding me, Hudson?"

"Sir, I know this is bad, but we've got a new operations director on this. De Boer."

"I don't give a shit who's in charge of this now. You've got a problem."

"I know, sir. To be fair, I have been sending you emails highlighting my concerns."

"Forget that for a moment. So the question is, How do we clean house?"

"I'd like to talk about that, sir. As you know, I haven't been happy with the fallout from the first two operations Stone was involved in. And this should have been a relatively straightforward takedown."

"Stone is not a relatively straightforward individual. You know that, I know that, everyone knows that."

"This is more than Stone, sir. I think we need to talk about the man in charge. Berenger."

A silence opened up down the line.

"What are you saying?"

"I'm saying that what's happened is not acceptable. And we need to find a solution. Nathan Stone has not just gone rogue. Twice. But he also knows where the bodies are buried. He must be eliminated."

"We can't get directly involved, Hudson."

"I disagree, sir. Besides, things have changed. Doing nothing is no longer an option."

Black sighed. "This is not good."

"We have to get involved. This is rapidly getting out of control. It's like a contagion."

"How do you propose to address these concerns?"

"Better to discuss it in person."

"When?"

"As soon as possible."

"I have a lot going on, Catherine. I can't just drop everything for this program."

"I'm not asking you to drop anything, sir. I just want to meet with you. And outline my plan."

"The plan has gone to fuck. I'll get back to you about a time to meet and discuss the Commission's charter. But in the meantime I want you to fix this mess."

The line went dead.

Eleven

Stone paddled the boat hard as he negotiated the tall wooden markers that kept boats from venturing into too-shallow water. Up ahead through the murky dawn was Buoy Key and its water-monitoring station.

"Do you even know where you're going?" Beatrice shouted.

"I got this. You calmed down a bit?"

"Yeah, out in a boat in the fucking Everglades in the darkness. Yeah, that'll calm me down. Why the hell are we out here?"

"We would have been sitting ducks if we'd stayed in Miami, trust me. Or stayed on the highway."

"Surely it's better to hide in a city, with all those people."

"It's very easy to find someone in a city. Surveillance cameras everywhere. Highways. Restaurants. Offices."

Stone pushed on. The waters here were shallow. And underneath was thick, deep mud. Easy to get stuck in if you weren't paying attention.

Then he saw a familiar marker downwind. He headed due east through a narrow channel.

The wind began to whip up the water. Stone paddled on as the small boat rocked back and forth in the choppy waters.

"I feel sick!" Beatrice said, holding her stomach.

"Be sick if you have to. Probably for the best. Get all the booze out too."

A few moments later the woman threw up over the side of the boat. "Shit," she said. "Sorry."

"Nothing to be sorry about. If you have to puke, then you have to puke."

"I must've lost my mind. When will this be over?"

"I'm working on it."

Stone checked his watch. On the far horizon the first pink tinges showed the new day. It would soon be dawn. He stopped paddling and rested for a minute.

Beatrice put her head over the side of the boat and was violently sick again. "Goddamn," she said.

"Better?"

She nodded and hunched forward, head in her hands.

"We need to get away from this channel before it gets light," he said.

Stone paddled a few hundred yards to the nearest key. He reached out for Beatrice, who was sitting hunched in the boat. "You need to get out."

"Here?"

"This is where we set up camp today."

Beatrice shook her head. "I don't want to go anywhere."

"Now!"

She gave him a wounded look, stepped off the boat barefoot, holding her shoes, and promptly sank ankle-deep in mud. "Oh fuck."

Stone jumped out and pulled the boat high up the muddy shoreline between the short, spiky mangrove trees that covered the small key. He left her to follow him.

Stone walked a few yards and pushed through the twisted mangrove trees until the greenery morphed into broad-leaved oak hammocks. It was a sign they were on slightly higher, sandy ground in the center of the tiny island.

Beatrice slumped down in the sand and curled into a ball.

Stone got busy. He took out his car keys, which had a Swiss Army knife attached.

"What are you doing?" she asked. "I can see the knife."

"Relax. We need shelter. For camouflage during the daytime but also to protect us from the sun. Agreed?"

"Sure."

"So, do you want to get with the program?"

"Do I have to?"

"This is to give us a chance. It's a matter of survival."

Beatrice got to her feet. "You want me to help?"

Stone nodded as he began to hack away at the branches with the knife. He wiped the sweat from his forehead with the back of his hand. A cotton-candy dawn washed over the Everglades as they set up their makeshift camp. Nathan cut down countless branches. He took two of them and cut them into spears. He handed one to Beatrice. "You could try and kill me with that if you want."

"Please don't joke about things like that."

"Listen, use it for protection. If you see a gator or something like that."

"Thanks for raising my spirits."

"It's mostly crocodiles in the Keys anyway. A few gators drawn by the freshwater tributaries. But they'll mostly ignore you as long as you stay away."

Beatrice wiped the sweat beading her brow. "Crocs and gators. Gee, thanks for reminding me that I must be out of my fucking mind."

Stone began to build a platform using branches. He showed Beatrice how to place palm fronds for bedding. Then he stuck sharpened branches into the earth and erected a primitive tent, using palm fronds again for cover.

"High ground, very important," he said.

Beatrice nodded.

"We need to be aware of our surroundings."

Beatrice lay down on the fronds, still holding the spear. "I feel ill. I'm scared. What the hell is happening?"

Stone didn't answer. He got to work starting a fire. He gathered bracken and some fibrous dry leaves from higher up on the trees. And some moss. Then he covered it all with dry sticks he cut into small strips.

His shirt was sticking to his back. He surrounded the fire with stones to stop it from spreading across the rest of the key.

He pulled out his Zippo lighter and blew into the dry moss until the flame caught. Then he added more twigs and branches.

"We're going to make it if we're smart," he said.

"I hope so. I want to get back to my goddamn family."

"You will." Stone looked at the fire. "This is only a start. But it's something."

Beatrice began to cry.

Twelve

Just after sunrise, Kevin de Boer was shielding his eyes from the harsh morning sun as he stood beside the SUV. They had pulled over onto a shoulder off the isolated road where his brother's GPS signal had last been located. They had been scouring the road back and forth for an hour. And he was worried sick that his brother hadn't been in touch.

De Boer felt a sense of foreboding wash over him. He couldn't bear to lose his brother. That would be too much for him.

A car sped past.

De Boer began to pace up and down. He took out his cell phone and called the secret operations room in the basement of a warehouse complex near Sarasota. Around the huge hangar-like space, dozens of intelligence operatives, military strategists, and computer experts would be working to figure out where Nathan Stone and the girl were. But his brother dropping off the radar had only added to his problems.

A young woman, a former staffer at the National Security Council who had just joined the team, answered the call. "Kevin, any luck on the ground?"

"Negative. Listen to me. Nathan Stone and my brother can't have just disappeared off the face of the earth," de Boer said. "We haven't had a visual on Stone for nearly five hours. It can't happen in this day and age. I'm not buying it."

"Sir, Florida is a big place."

"My brother said he was near Homestead. We are on the Main Park Road, which leads out of there. We've been up and down it. Nothing. There must be surveillance cameras even down here."

"There really aren't. They're mostly in cities and towns. Miami. Fort Lauderdale. Highways."

De Boer shielded his eyes as the sun beat down. He felt the sweat plastering his shirt to his back. "Where's the new cyberguy? Has he arrived?"

"I'll put him on, sir."

A beat. A tentative voice came down the line. "Morning, sir."

"When did you arrive?"

"Twenty minutes ago. Just flew in from Seattle. Been hooking up our cloud systems."

"Right. You know the brief?"

"Find Nathan Stone. Find the girl. Right?"

"And my brother too."

"Got it."

"There's a lot riding on this. Do you understand what I'm saying?"

"I'm assuming you mean national security threats."

"Precisely. These two are national security threats. I can't give you the lowdown on who and what they are. Suffice it to say they are a danger to America, its interests, and those of its allies. Am I making myself clear?"

The kid gave a nervous cough. "Sir, I'll hopefully have a better picture of what we're facing within the hour."

"Good. Because so far we have come up with nothing. They've dropped off the grid. How is that even possible? It's impossible."

"Long story short, sir, but yeah, it's possible."

"Are we scanning surveillance cameras belonging to the FBI, Miami-Dade Police, Miami Beach, across the city and beyond?"

"That's all in place. I've uploaded some great new facial recognition software too. But it takes time. It's very precise. High degree of accuracy."

De Boer felt a wave of exhaustion wash over him. He hadn't slept in twenty-four hours. "Right, so you're on this. Highway cameras, we're into them?"

"We're in. We're scanning in real time all footage since these two dropped off the grid."

"I want us to go deeper. That should be just the starting point."

"What do you mean, sir?"

"I want to get into each and every webcam, private surveillance systems, I want to get into everything. Everywhere."

The kid whistled. "Interesting. You do know that's totally illegal, I'm assuming, not to mention an extraordinarily complex technical operation?"

"Son," he said, "I don't want to know if something is going to be tough to implement. And I sure as hell don't want a lecture about what is and isn't legal."

"Sir, I wasn't suggesting . . . It's just that I wanted to make clear how challenging that would be. It's not straightforward."

"We need to find this guy. He is a danger to national security, and so is the girl. American national security. I'm assuming you believe in national security."

"Hell yeah."

"Of course you do. Now listen, this is not a drill. Not a training exercise. This is the real thing."

The kid sighed. "I get that. Four people, including me, are working on this. But what you're suggesting is, you want every device, cell phone, surveillance system, private and public, in and around Miami to come into our orbit. Do you have any idea what you're asking?"

"I want the area around Homestead covered. Hell, I want Florida covered."

"Florida? Florida is a big-ass state, sir, with respect. That's a big ask."

"That's why I called you guys. You do stuff like this, don't you?"

"We're the best. We've advised the UN on cybersecurity, NATO, the CIA, you name it."

"So let's get to work. I want a dragnet like you wouldn't believe. Stone is dangerous. But we don't know where he is. So how do we find him?"

The kid cleared his throat. "To be clear, you are instructing me to use any method, legal or illegal, to track them down."

"Precisely. Can you live with that?"

"Sure."

De Boer looked a few hundred yards farther down the road and saw Roel Bakker signaling him. "Do what you need to do. I want results."

He ended the call. He got back in the SUV and was driven a couple of hundred yards to where Bakker, red-faced and sweating, was standing in a ditch by the road. He got out. "What is it?"

Bakker bent down and pointed out bloodstains on the grassy mud and fragments of plastic. "Visor?"

De Boer's stomach knotted.

Bakker showed him broken branches of trees. "It's all trampled down just a few yards from the bloodstains."

De Boer took a few steps to the bloodstains. "Christ." He pushed through the trees and tall grass, squelching in the dirt. Farther and farther from the road. A few moments later, he saw the twisted handlebars of the bike shrouded in long grass. Then he saw the black leather jacket. He pushed back the grass to reveal his brother's body.

Thirteen

Stone was reaching up to cut the highest of the vine's branches as the setting sun spread a golden glow across the waters all around. They'd slept most of the day in the shelter, but soon it would be time to move again. He made a second cut at the bottom of the vine. Then he tipped the dripping water into an empty bean can that had washed up onto the tiny key they were holed up on.

He cut a dozen more vines in a similar manner and poured the contents into assorted other beer cans that had washed up.

Stone then heated the cans on the fire. After they had cooled slightly, he called across to Beatrice, who seemed to have calmed down a notch after her meltdown. "You need to carefully fill up all those empty plastic bottles with this water. It's clean. Warm but clean."

"That doesn't look good."

"It's fine. It's pure. Not chilled, I'll grant you. But it will keep you alive."

"I'm so dehydrated I need some now."

"Let's get all these bottles filled up to keep us going for the next twenty-four hours. Then we can hydrate."

Beatrice nodded. "The guy you shot . . . he was really going to kill us?"

"No question about it. Now, let's think how we should move forward."

Beatrice sat in silence.

Stone looked at her. He actually felt strangely sorry for the woman. She was trying to put a brave face on things. Despite bleeding from all the bites from the bugs and mosquitos, she seemed more in control of her emotions. He watched as she poured the water from the cans very carefully into the plastic bottles. The fact that she looked so much like his sister—the sunken eyes, the tired smile—he found oddly comforting. The way she rolled her eyes—Helen did the same thing. It was uncanny. She was vulnerable too. And he felt strangely protective of her. The way he felt for his sister.

"You're doing really well," he said.

Beatrice turned and flashed him a beautiful smile. "What's gotten into you?"

"I want you to know I'll protect you. Whatever it takes, all of this doesn't have anything to do with you. I understand that. And I will do what has to be done. That's all I want you to know."

"Thank you. That means a lot."

"Take five of the bottles," he said, taking off his shirt, "and wrap them up in this shirt so they don't spill out. And, obviously, keep them all upright. You okay?"

Beatrice nodded. "Sure. I think I got this."

"Look, I'm sorry for the gun at your head and everything."

Beatrice dropped her gaze. "Don't let it happen again."

"It was fight or flight. We needed to get out of Miami. Get away from civilization."

"Well, we certainly achieved that."

Beatrice picked up the bottles, two in each hand, carried them down to the small boat, then loaded up the rest. She made sure to wrap them tight and upright with Stone's shirt.

Stone handed her another bottle of warm water. "Here, drink this."

Beatrice sniffed it. "Are you sure it's okay?"

Stone gulped his own bottle down. "See. It's warm but clean. It's good."

Beatrice did the same. "That was surprisingly good."

Stone wiped his mouth with the back of his hand. "That's better."

Beatrice closed her eyes for a moment. "This is way too much reality for my liking."

"Reality, huh?"

"I'm an actress. I live in Santa Monica. This is not how I live."

"It's a bit uncomfortable, I understand. And the stuff with me pressing a gun to your head, what can I say? I'm sorry."

Beatrice folded her arms. "Well, I've been carjacked before in West Hollywood, so that wasn't anything new."

Stone gave a wry smile. "Now, that is a crazy place, I'll give you that."

"What's the plan?"

Stone sighed. "The plan? The plan is to stay alive. We have water. We're hidden. For now. But we need to keep on moving. Probably for the next twenty-four hours. And then we'll try and get back to civilization. Think you can handle that?"

"So we're going to be out here for another day, with the bugs and humidity, in the middle of absolutely nowhere?"

"Pretty much."

"I need to know more. I'm still freaking out."

"What do you need to know? You're alive."

"I get that. But I need to know what this is all about. Really about."

"You don't want to know, trust me."

"I think I've got a right to know. You said you were an assassin. And you killed a guy somewhere overseas?"

"Among others."

"This is fucked up, I have to tell you."

Stone said nothing.

"You've had opportunities to kill me in the past twelve hours. Headed down that mosquito-infested trail. And you didn't."

Stone nodded.

"It's like you knew where you were going."

"I do."

"So you've been down that dirt track before?"

"It's called Snake Bight Trail, if you must know."

"Right. You could've killed me on the boat. And you could've killed me in this godforsaken place. So why haven't you?"

"I don't want to. I don't have to. That's why."

"I just don't know what I've gotten myself involved in. Why? Why are they so intent on killing you?"

"I don't know if I should talk about it, to be honest." Stone shook his head. "It shouldn't have gotten this crazy, I know that."

Beatrice nodded.

"I can't tell you much. I did a hit in Europe. I can't say who it was. I was kept in isolation at a facility off the northwest coast of Scotland. And from there I was released onto the mainland and told to kill a guy."

Beatrice ran a hand through her hair, working out a tangle. "Can't you say any more?"

Stone shook his head.

"Can't or won't?"

"There's a lot of stuff you wouldn't understand."

"Try me."

"I kill people. And I killed a few people, powerful people, in New York. That's why this has escalated so badly."

"I don't like this. I don't like any of this. I don't want any part of it."

"That's understandable. You've stumbled inadvertently into a world most people probably don't know exists. Assassinations. Murders made to look like accidents. Neutralizing people."

"Shit." She stared at the ground, eyes wide, for a moment. Then she looked up at Stone. "That's disgusting, you know? You kill people? Who does that?"

"Our government does it every day. On your behalf."

"I'd like to know who you killed. Neutralized, whatever you call it."

"Why?"

"Why? I just do. Morbid curiosity, I guess."

"If I tell you, it will almost certainly put you at risk."

"From you?"

"Not from me. From them. The people who want to kill me. The people who hired you."

Beatrice folded her arms. "You say I'm already at risk from them?"

"You are."

"Then you might as well tell me. Who did you kill?"

"If we make it out of here, I might tell you. How about that? But revealing that information to anyone else would not be a smart move for you, believe me."

"So, they want to silence you and me?"

Stone turned and saw that the sky was darkening, turning bloodred. "We need to move pretty soon while there's still some light."

"Answer me. They want to silence us both?"

"They do now. They absolutely want to kill me. But they'll want to get rid of you too. Any further questions?"

"I want to get out of here. I'm scared."

"I understand."

"Do you? Do you know what I'm going through?"

"I can imagine."

"You can imagine . . . I just have a feeling that you're going to kill me. I can't get over it."

"Why would I kill you?"

"I don't know. Because that's what you do?"

Stone shook his head. "I don't blame you for thinking like that. But the real threat to you is from the people who hired you."

"I can't imagine that this is going to end well."

"It won't if we stay still. We need to go now."

"Go where?"

"Another key. About a mile southeast of here."

"Why the hell did you bring us out here? Aren't we an easy target?" She turned in a circle. "No cops. No witnesses." She gestured to the sticks he'd sharpened, lying on the ground near the tent. "I bet they have better weapons than we do."

"We need to avoid cities. Civilization. Surveillance. I explained this already."

Beatrice sat down on the dirt, swatting away the bugs that were starting to thicken the air. "You said I could leave. But it wasn't the right time. Is this the right time?"

"No, because you would die out here by yourself. But if your question is, Would I stop you? The answer is no."

"So I can go?"

Stone pointed to the boat. "Take it. It's yours. If you want it."

"Can you take me back to the trail?"

"No. That's not where I'm going. I'm heading southeast. Through the outer Keys and back to civilization."

"And if you don't make it?"

"I believe I will. If I go back the way we came, they will find us. For sure."

Beatrice scratched her head. "Goddamn bugs."

"They're everywhere here. Listen, if you want, you can take the boat."

"What about you?"

"What about me?"

"What are you going to do? Are you going to just let me go?"

"You wanna go? Then go."

"You really think those people will kill me?"

Stone sighed. "If you manage to make it back—and that's a big if—you will be interviewed by the cops. You will give your real name, your stage name, whatever. And then they will know where you are. And they will wait. The police will take you to the hospital for a checkup. Chances are you won't make it out of the hospital alive."

"You're just trying to scare me."

"You're not my problem. *They* are my problem. And now they're your problem too."

"And you're not going to kill me or harm me in any way?"

"I want to get the hell out of here as much as you do. But we need to be smart to try and evade these people. And heading back the way we came, back into civilization, is not smart. When we resurface, we need to be well away from there."

"So, we're going to another island like this . . ."

"It's a bit bigger. I've been out here before. I know about survival. And I can tell you this: I would be better off without you tagging along. So I'm prepared to let you go. If that's what you want."

"I want to live. That's what I want."

"Then you have to make up your mind. Am I a danger to you?"

Beatrice looked up at the darkening sky as if for inspiration. "I don't know."

"You need to decide."

"No . . . I don't think you're a danger to me."

Stone nodded. "All right then. Let's get back in the boat. We have water now and we'll head off to another key." He held out his hand and she grabbed it. Stone pulled her to her feet.

"Look at me, I'm disgusting," she said. "I cannot wait to get someplace where I can take a shower."

"Well, don't hold your breath just yet."

Stone kicked sand onto the fire and they headed to the boat through twisted mangroves until they got to the sandy shoreline. He pushed off as she clambered in beside the bottles of water. Egrets were silhouetted against the inky-blue sky. He paddled hard for a few hundred yards, then the paddle caught in the mud in the shallow waters. "Fuck," he said before he managed to wrench it free.

Swarms of bugs filled the air. Nathan saw an alligator on a sand-bank a few yards away and was grateful Beatrice didn't notice. They continued past the mangrove-fringed islands and into deeper channels.

"How far?" she asked.

"Fifteen, twenty minutes."

Stone turned down yet another narrow channel, forcing the oar through the muddy shallows, through seagrass, the paddle getting twisted among the reeds. His eyes were adjusting to the stygian dark-ness. He pressed on, paddling hard, arms pumping.

Nearly half an hour later, an island came into view in the far dis-tance. A bigger key, covered in mangroves, live oaks on a higher eleva-tion, and thick vegetation.

Stone brought them closer and closer. He paddled up to the sandy shoreline, jumped off, and dragged the boat up high like before. Beatrice handed him the bottles of water, which he placed in the sand. Then he helped her out of the boat.

Beatrice picked up the bottles and followed Stone silently along a well-worn muddy trail. Finally, he pushed through a thick mangrove canopy to the sandy center of the island. A small, rudimentary wooden cabin stood in the middle.

"What the hell?" she said.

"This was built about ten years ago by a friend of mine. Lived on the Keys for a while. Former Marine."

"Out here? Are you kidding me?"

Stone swatted away some mosquitos. "Got evicted from his house and he headed out here and built this. Lived here for a few months every winter."

"Fuck. Is this for real?"

Stone pushed open the creaking door. Inside was a dark space, mostly empty aside from a twin bed. He spotted a cupboard and opened it. Inside were cans of bug spray, citronella candles, and some crackers. He handed her a can of bug spray.

Beatrice sprayed it on her body and all around.

"You okay?" he said.

"Not really. But I don't feel as far from civilization here, if that makes sense."

Stone lit the candles, and light washed over the dark interior of the hut. "This will discourage a lot of the mosquitos from hanging out in and around here," he said. "At least that's what my friend found."

"It's real buggy," she said, spraying the chemicals on the bed.

Stone placed the bottles of water in the cupboard. He handed one to her. "Go on, drink."

Beatrice said, "I must be out of my freaking mind." She gulped down the warm water. "Tastes funny. Funky. It's not Evian, that's for sure."

Stone gave her a sleeve of crackers, and she scoffed five in quick succession. "That good?" he said.

Beatrice nodded. "My blood sugar levels were plummeting. Always get grouchy if I'm hungry." She looked around. "So you mind telling me what the deal is with this friend of yours?"

"My friend survived out here for months by himself. He started from scratch. You can handle one night."

Beatrice sat down on the bed. "I feel like screaming. But what good would that do?"

Stone kneeled down beside her and held her hand. "Sometimes you need to dig deep and be strong. That's all I'm asking from you. You can do this. You might feel like you're in hell, but trust me, you're not. Not by a long shot."

Beatrice nodded. "I'm just very scared. I feel alone."

"Think of this. You could scream all night and no one would hear you. Out here, not a living soul can hear you. Isolation can be liberating too."

Beatrice swatted away a mosquito. She looked at him, her eyes filling with tears. "I'm hanging on by a thread. I'm so tired I feel like I'm going to die. And I'm stuck out here with a guy who kills people for a living. I'm fucking scared."

Stone nodded. "You're not in your safe space?"

"Fuck you." But she laughed.

"I promise, Beatrice McNally, I want to get you back to where you're from. But you've got to trust me. We need to be resourceful. And we need to work as a team to get back to civilization."

Beatrice nodded.

"Do you trust me?"

Beatrice looked up at Nathan, tears in her eyes. "I don't know. I'm not a naturally trusting person. People let me down. They lie. They cheat. They hurt."

"You need to trust me. Can you trust me?"

"I guess I'll find out soon enough."

Fourteen

It was a long night in the sweltering makeshift shelter on the key. Stone lay on the uneven wooden floor while Beatrice tossed and turned on the bed. The citronella candle surrounded them with its sickly chemical scent, but it seemed to keep most of the mosquitos at bay.

Stone stared at the rough wooden ceiling. He thought about the days and weeks and months that his friend had spent alone in this space. He thought about the loneliness, the desperation that would lead someone to head to such a place. But in a way, Nathan admired the fact that the guy had claimed a little piece of America for his own. Most of the tiny islands were owned by the government and designated for wildlife preservation. Others were owned by wealthy individuals. Stone had once read that there were nearly a thousand islands in the Keys. But only around forty or so were occupied.

He imagined what the early pioneers headed west must have endured. Blistering heat. No mosquito repellants. No air-conditioning. No nothing. Just the desire to live free. To strive. To fight. To endure the unendurable. To put down roots. To live and die as free men and women with their own bit of land.

Stone had always admired that pioneering spirit. The indomitable resilience and desire to survive. He remembered as a boy, in the shithole one-room dive he called home, reading *The Call of the Wild* by Jack

London. He had read it over and over again, eager to find out what was going to happen to Buck, the dog that was stolen and had to survive in the rugged wilderness of Alaska. He marveled at the way Buck had to fight to stay alive. Then Buck had begun to dominate the other dogs.

Stone had always felt like an outsider. Someone who had to fight to survive, just like the dog. Fight on the streets when neighborhood bullies threw their weight around the old Lower East Side. Feral, wild beasts, just like Buck had become.

"Are you awake?" Beatrice's voice snapped him out of his reverie.

"Yeah."

"I'm being eaten alive."

"It could be worse, trust me."

"Why aren't you getting bitten?"

"I am. Stuff like that doesn't bother me."

"I stink too. I haven't showered in an age."

Stone sighed, exasperated. "You've got to learn to roll with it."

"I like being clean."

He smiled. "Who doesn't?"

"What's so funny?"

"First-world problems, right?"

"Jimmy, I wish you wouldn't make light of this. I am literally freaking out, and you're making jokes."

"It's a good defense mechanism. You need to learn that."

"Do you mind me asking a few questions?"

"Depends what it is you want to know."

"I was told you're from New York. Was all that stuff about the Lower East Side true?"

"Yeah, that's where I'm from. Bowery. And that was when it was pretty rough and scary. Not like now."

"And you and your sister grew up there?"

"We did."

"I lived in New York for a few years."

"You did? Whereabouts?"

"Up on the West Side."

"Nice part of town."

"I attended Juilliard."

Stone whistled. "That where you learned to act?"

"Yeah, pretty much. Won an acting scholarship."

"Good for you."

"Don't make fun. It was my dream since I was a little girl."

"Bet you weren't ever taught how to survive out in the Everglades with a trained killer, though, were you?"

"There you go again. I don't think you have any idea how you come across."

"I don't worry about things like that."

"Well, maybe you should."

"Look, I'm sorry. I know you're upset about what's going on. Where I come from and what I've been taught, empathy was never my thing."

"Lower East Side have a part in that?"

"Yeah, along with my father. He was a bastard."

"My mother was the bane of my existence."

Stone contemplated his fleeting memories of his own mother for a few moments. He wondered where she was at that moment. Was she still out there somewhere, waiting for him? He hoped so.

"I don't think I ever went to the Lower East Side," Beatrice said, cutting into his thoughts.

"You kidding me?"

"No. You believe that?"

"It's changed from when I grew up."

"I used to go to clubs and bars in the East Village. That was pretty edgy back in the day. Avenue D for death, right?"

"I know that area well. Still a bit sketchy out on Avenue D." Stone sighed. His mind flashed to images of him and his sister crammed into their one-room apartment on the Bowery, dreading the return of their psychotic, drunken father. He let himself remember the beatings. The excruciating pain as his father's leather belt lashed his puny body, his hands up, trying to defend his face. He sometimes wished he could have defended his sister. The reality was that she had been the one defending him, killing their father. If he had been bigger and older, he would have gotten his sister out of there before it was too late.

"I miss New York. I moved out west thinking I was going to make it in movies. Guess I was wrong."

"You might one day. Life is never a straight line."

"That's true. That is so fucking true it's not real. But directors are looking for younger women. Girls, ideally. High cheekbones."

"Hollywood is a crazy place, or so I've heard. You have to be strong to make it there."

"You better believe it. I've gone on auditions where I've been asked to strip naked, have sex with a casting director, give blow jobs to all manner of scumbags. I told them all to go to hell."

"Good for you. You have to have integrity."

"Hollywood? Integrity? They're all sharks. And the ones that aren't get eaten alive. It's not for the fainthearted. The number of friends I've had who ended up drug addicts, suicides, or flat-out crazy after trying to earn a living in Hollywood is no laughing matter."

"Shit. Makes my line of work look tame."

"Everyone is obviously desperate for parts. We're all holding down three or four jobs and heading to auditions when we can. It's insane. And it's always promises, promises."

"What do you mean?"

"I've lost count of the number of times people have made promises about parts or auditions. And it was just bullshit. Managers, agents—everyone just wants their slice."

Stone listened but said nothing. He didn't know anything about the film world. Or actors.

"I thought I had hit rock bottom in LA. But this is just batshit crazy. Can't believe I'm holed up in such a pit."

"Trust me, I've been in worse."

"You gotta be kidding me."

"Nope."

"Where?"

"My home."

"In New York?"

"When I say home, it was really a room. A stinking room. Cockroaches, mice, and occasionally rats crawling inside the walls. Sometime inside the room. We were filthy. So, when you say this is the pits, trust me, this ain't."

"I'm sorry."

"Hey, what doesn't kill you makes you stronger, right?"

"Or crazy."

Stone sighed, knowing that was what had happened to his sister.

"I'm sorry, I'm saying the wrong thing again. Shit. I'm an idiot, sorry."

"You don't have to say sorry. It is what it is. But we got out of there. Thanks to my sister."

"How did you get out? Did you guys sneak out in the night?"

"My sister killed my father with a pair of scissors. He was drunk and beating on us. I couldn't protect us. And she took matters into her hands."

"That's so awful."

"My one regret is that I couldn't protect her and deal with it myself. The fact is I owe her my life. She sacrificed her freedom and probably her sanity to save both of us."

"You said that they, the people who hired me, kidnapped your sister."

"That was a year ago or so. They took her from a psychiatric hospital. She's a paranoid schizophrenic, I think. Drugs control some of the symptoms."

"Is she okay now?"

Stone sighed. "It's a struggle for her. She looks a lot like you, actually. But she's got a different temperament."

"How so?"

"She's very placid. The drugs have made her that way. And her condition."

"I'm sorry."

"I don't like talking about her."

"Why not?"

Stone closed his eyes, wishing Beatrice would just fall asleep.

"You know, it's okay to talk about things. Things that hurt us."

"I'd rather not."

"Why not? My therapist says it's vital to be open and bring out our thoughts and desires."

Nathan was silent.

"If you don't want to talk about it, that's fine. I'm cool with that."

"What about you?"

"What about me?"

"Where you from? I mean really from?"

"Midwest. Small town. You wouldn't know it. My dad left when I was a kid. And my mom, who was also an aspiring actress, decided we needed to move to Long Island. Then she married a lawyer and I moved out."

"Tough."

"I live on the beach now. One-bedroom apartment. Loud neighbors. But it's not bad if you want to go to auditions but also work in bars and restaurants. A girl's gotta live." She swatted a couple of mosquitos. "Goddamn!"

"This ain't Rodeo Drive."

"Where I live sure isn't Rodeo Drive, let me tell you. That's up in Beverly Hills. Don't be so goddamn snarky."

"You need to understand how much worse things could be. I find that helps."

"What do you mean?"

"Well, can you imagine no light? No repellent?"

Beatrice went quiet.

"You know who used to occupy this area? Who used to live out here for generations?"

"Who?"

"The Seminole."

Beatrice cleared her throat and swatted another bug.

"They survived out here because they had to. The government tried to force them out of Florida, and so they ran into the Everglades, which would offer them protection. Or so they thought."

"And how did that work out for them, huh?"

"They survived. For a while. Bet they never taught you that at Juilliard."

Beatrice sighed. "You want to ease up on me a little? I'm feeling kinda fragile."

"We need to be tough to get out of here. You've got to use your brains. Live off your wits." Stone got up and took a bottle of water from the cupboard. He handed it to her. "Important to keep hydrated."

Beatrice sat up and drank two-thirds of the bottle. She handed it back. "I didn't realize how thirsty I was."

Stone finished the rest. He got another bottle and handed her that. She took a few gulps and he finished the rest. "Better?"

Beatrice smiled. "Now I need to pee."

"There's a latrine outside."

"The hole in the ground?"

"That's it."

She groaned as she got up. She went outside. He heard her peeing. A few minutes later, she was back inside. "That's disgusting." She lay down on the bed. "I want to know more about you."

"I think I've said enough."

"You killed a guy overseas. Who?"

Stone sighed, not wanting to engage in that subject. "You don't want to go there."

"I do. Besides, if I don't make it out of here, what does it matter?"

"I'm working on the assumption that we will get out of here. You don't need to know this stuff."

"Jimmy . . . I don't even know if you're telling me the truth. You talk about trust. Well, I've told you what I know about all this. About me being hired."

"I appreciate that."

"But you haven't really told me anything."

"That's not true. I told you about what I do. About why these people want me dead. About growing up in New York. About my sister."

Beatrice went quiet for a moment. "You know what I thought might happen?"

"What?"

"Thought you'd just kill me here tonight. I was petrified. Can you imagine that?"

"Like I said before, you're free to take the boat. Chances are if you took the boat and headed out, someone would spot you. And you would be fine. For a while."

Beatrice was quiet for a moment as she thought that over. She turned onto her side. "I need to know who you killed. I sense that it's someone famous. I need to know."

Stone chuckled. "Maybe another day."

"Come on. Twenty questions. How did you kill whoever it was?"

"I used a weapon that induces a heart attack."

"Are you shitting me?"

"No."

"And this was in Europe?"

"Yes, that's where he was."

"Why?"

"That's what I do. I kill people."

"You kill people? Plural? So I'm shacked up with a serial killer?"

"I'm not a serial killer. A serial killer kills and tortures for his own gratification. I kill for money. I kill because my government tells me to. Because a private organization thinks a man, or woman, has too much influence and is working against their interests."

"How do you feel about that?"

"I hadn't really considered my feelings, to be honest. It's not something that bothers me."

"Maybe you should think about it."

Stone said nothing, just stretched out some more, hands behind his head, knuckles touching the rough wooden floor.

"How can you live with yourself?"

"I know what I am. And what I do. And it's not nice."

"All my instincts say to run. To hide from you. But here I am, sleeping underneath the same roof as you."

The shriek of a wild animal disturbed the quiet outside.

"What the fuck was that?" Beatrice asked, sitting up suddenly.

"Maybe a panther."

"They have panthers out here?"

"A lot of wildlife out here. Maybe it was from an island downwind."

"And we're not at risk?"

Stone shrugged. "I've got a Glock. That might help."

"Don't be so cavalier. So what's your middle name? Jimmy what?"

"Not important."

Beatrice ran her fingers through her hair. "My daughter will be missing me."

"You said your ex is looking after her."

Beatrice nodded. "He's an actor too."

Stone said nothing.

"My life's been shit for years, to be honest. I mean, down the fucking toilet in luck and love. He was mean too."

"How?"

"I'd rather not go there. Took me two years of expensive therapy to try and put that behind me. He said I was a bad mother."

"Were you?"

"I wasn't the best."

"Why not?"

"Is this you judging me? Is that what this is?"

"I'm just asking you a question. Don't get so touchy."

"I'd leave her in the apartment by herself when I went on auditions. When I went to work in a bar. Satisfied?"

"How old was she at the time?"

"Ten. Eleven."

"You gotta do what you gotta do, right?"

Beatrice sighed. "That's what I thought. We lived separate lives. But my husband always berated me about it. He got some private investigator to take pictures of my daughter alone, answering the door to the mailman. Then we divorced and he decided to take her with him, until he got bored with her. She stayed with me for a few weeks when he got a new girlfriend. But then the girlfriend left him, and my daughter went back to my ex."

Stone said nothing. He knew all about dysfunctional parents. But this woman's idea of dysfunctional and his were polar opposites. "Why are you beating yourself up? You didn't abandon her."

Beatrice shook her head. "No, I didn't."

"Did you beat her?"

"Never." She sat partway up. "And neither did my ex, by the way. I'd never have left her with him if he had. But I did neglect her sometimes. She had to survive alone in our little apartment."

"But at least she was close to the beach."

"There are a lot of creeps hanging around. I should've looked out for her better. I was self-centered. Self-obsessed. Still am. Well, at least that's what my ex says."

Stone felt sorry for her in a way. He didn't feel sorry for anyone usually. "Life's tough."

"He said I neglected her. Neglected? That was like a dagger through the heart."

"Trust me, I know all about neglect. What your daughter experienced was not neglect."

Beatrice sighed and shrugged. "Are you married?"

Stone shook his head.

"What about girlfriends?"

"None that I can remember."

"Fuck. Ever?"

Stone said nothing.

"Have you ever been in therapy?"

"Do I look like I've been in therapy?"

"I guess not."

Beatrice was staring at Stone as if examining his profile.

"What are you looking at?"

"You."

"You wanna knock it off?"

"Why? You've got an interesting face."

"Okay, enough talking about faces."

"What's the problem with talking about your face? Yeah, maybe you need a shave. But other than that, why the hell are you so touchy?"

"I don't want to talk about it."

Beatrice yawned. "It's going to be a long night."

"Try and get some sleep, then. We're on the move at first light."

"You're not going to kill me?"

Stone didn't answer, just let himself drift away, the sound of her chattering like white noise in his head.

Fifteen

Berenger was floating on a dark river, feeling his head dip under the water, black skies above. He awoke on the Gulfstream bathed in cold sweat, his cell phone ringing. He took a moment to gather himself as he glanced at his phone beside the bed.

The caller ID said it was de Boer. The LCD showed it was 5:21 a.m. local time.

Berenger reached over and answered. "Kevin, just wanted to say again, I'm so sorry about Pieter. If you want to hand over the reins, I'll understand."

"Not a chance. Plenty of time to grieve."

"I respect that."

"Mark, I think we might have something."

"What?"

"I'm just going to send you an encrypted message. Call me back when you've seen it."

A beep signaled the end of the call.

Berenger navigated to his encrypted email and clicked on the message from de Boer. It opened, and footage immediately began to play. It had been taken with a night-vision camera, not high quality. The footage was slow and jerky. Then the clip ended. The image frozen on the screen showed what looked like Nathan Stone and the woman crouched amid a grove of mangroves, about to climb onto a small boat.

Berenger felt his heart rate quicken. He called de Boer. "Talk to me, Kevin. What the hell is this?"

"The cyberteam we brought in unearthed this. They're unbelievable. We should have had them here from the start. They've been running their own facial recognition software, seemingly the most advanced there is, through every wireless surveillance camera in Florida."

"Every one?"

"Every goddamn one."

"Jesus Christ."

"And guess what? It's picked them up."

"You want to explain this to me in layman's terms? How was this image captured exactly?"

"A motion-activated, ultraviolet, night-vision camera deep in the southern Everglades."

"The Everglades? Who put the camera in place?"

"This is where it gets interesting. It was set up by a wildlife conservation charity, Everglades Evermore, and it captured this image of Stone and the woman just over eight hours ago, just after sunset."

"Where was this image captured?"

"We have the coordinates. It's an uninhabited key. Four nautical miles from the trail where we believe they entered the Everglades, then stole this boat."

Berenger clenched his fist in triumph. He looked out the Gulfstream window at the clouds below. "That's terrific work. I don't want to waste any time. Let's get our teams into place."

"I've got a couple of tracking experts, survival experts too, on the way."

"It's not so straightforward to find them from here, I assume."

"It's gonna be tough. Stone is an expert. And he can survive just about any place in the world, any environment. Don't get me wrong, he'll find it hard going too."

"I can't understand why the woman is there. What is that all about?"

"I don't know if he's taken her hostage, thinking she might come in handy."

"It'll slow him down. I don't understand why he didn't leave her by the side of the road or just neutralize her."

"Maybe he already has."

"Fuck," Berenger snapped. "Why the hell didn't we just take him out in cold blood outside that bar?"

"Why indeed. A lesson for everyone, I guess."

Berenger sighed. "Let's get in there. Let's find them. And this time no fuck-ups."

Sixteen

Stone had barely slept. He popped a couple of steroid-and-amphetamine pills into his mouth and ground them with his teeth. He checked his watch. It was four a.m. Beatrice was sleeping. Breathing deep and gentle. He looked across at her. He needed to move now. Unhindered by someone who wasn't used to living in such conditions.

The more he thought about it, the more he realized he needed to leave her there. He could move on. No ties. It made sense. Someone would find her. Eventually. But it could be days. Weeks. No one would hear her scream out there.

The easiest thing to do would be to just leave the hut, head down to the boat, and push off. The Nathan Stone of old wouldn't have batted an eye. He would have been gone. Without a word. Then again, the Nathan Stone of old could just as easily have put a bullet in her head.

So why the hell wasn't he doing that now?

It was like he had changed in the last year. It was like something had been rekindled within him. Deep within his soul, a part of him that he thought was gone, a part of him that he thought had been destroyed was alive. The part that still retained a semblance of what it was like to be a human being. A man. Slowly it was beginning to dawn on him that he cared about the woman sleeping a few feet from him.

The people who were after him would certainly kill her. They didn't fuck around.

Stone reflected on his position and what he could intuit about the current management of the Commission. He thought about the psychiatrist who had examined him. Evaluated him. In Scotland. And in Canada. Berenger had examined Helen too when they'd kidnapped her. He knew the buttons that could be pressed. Had Beatrice, a woman who looked so much like Helen, been chosen by Berenger to approach Nathan in the bar simply because of her striking similarity to his sister? Did Berenger believe the resemblance would allow Nathan, perhaps subconsciously, to drop his guard?

Stone thought back to his numerous sessions with Berenger. He'd sensed the psychologist's innate fear of him. He'd observed how Berenger's gaze dropped if Stone gave him a long, cold stare. But he'd also noticed how fascinated Berenger was with him. The psychiatrist had liked to linger over the telling of brutal episodes in Stone's life. Perhaps most of all, he'd fixated on Stone's upbringing. His mother. His father. He'd wanted to know what triggered Stone. Berenger seemed to savor Stone's stories about his father's beatings. He wanted to know how Stone had evolved from being bullied on the streets and at home to being able to fight back. To no longer feeling the fear.

Beatrice stirred for a moment, snapping Stone out of his thoughts.

Stone watched her, bathed in the glow from the candles. Her breathing was shallow. His gut told him to move. Leave now. The men working for the Commission were smart people. Dangerous. They would have picked up his trail by now. And there was too much at stake for them to allow Stone or the girl to live.

Stone had the ability to disappear. She didn't. She would die if he didn't help her. Was that his problem? He didn't want to abandon her to her fate. But then again, what about his sister? His sister's fate depended on him making it out of this alive. It might not be safe for him to return to Florida to see her for a while, but he could still keep in touch from afar. And eventually, when it was safe, he could move her to somewhere they'd never find her.

Stone looked at the woman's reddened face, seared by the sun and mottled with insect bites. He saw the way her hair was matted to her face with sweat, flushed just the way Helen's face was when she got angry. He closed his eyes. His life was all about compartmentalization. He lived alone. He didn't rely on anyone. He didn't need anyone. He didn't want anyone in his life. He couldn't remember a time when he'd truly felt anything. It was only Helen he cared about. And even that was in a state of total detachment. He still didn't feel a real connection. To her. To anyone.

The boy he'd been had grown not into a man but a monster. A cold killing machine, trained and deployed first by the American army, then by the CIA. But now, faced with abandoning a woman he didn't really know and to whom he owed nothing, he was hesitant, indecisive. Stricken by doubt. That had never been a problem in the past. He was asked to kill, then he killed. He tasted blood each and every day. And felt no remorse at what he had become.

So what was stopping him now from disappearing into the night?

Stone rubbed his face. He felt strange. It was almost like something deep within him, something that had lain buried, dormant since it had been beaten out of him as a boy, was beginning to stir. The ability to feel. To understand. To care. An essential part of being a human being. It was like the walls he had built around himself for protection were now allowing a small ray of light into his dark soul.

Beatrice stirred again and bolted upright, bathed in sweat. Her eyes found the glow of Stone's in the waning candlelight. "Were you watching me?"

Stone nodded. "Watching over you."

"I see. How long was I asleep for?"

"A couple of hours, I think."

"Did you sleep?"

"For a little while," he lied.

"Feel like I'm burning up," she said.

Stone got up and handed her a bottle of the cloudy vine water. "Drink it."

"Thanks." She winced as she swallowed, then handed the bottle to Stone. He finished the rest. "So," she said, looking around, "you weren't tempted to kill me?"

"Not yet," he said, cracking a smile.

Beatrice closed her eyes. "Gimme strength." She picked up her bag and reached inside. "I must be a mess."

"You look okay to me."

"I'll take that as a compliment," she said, using a perfumed wipe to take her mascara and makeup off. "I'm alive. It's something."

"Are you still scared of me?"

"A little bit. Feel like I've been sucked into my own personal hell."

"Know what Churchill said?"

Beatrice shrugged.

"If you're going through hell, keep going."

She nodded. "Makes sense."

"You've got a choice. You can still go back."

"Or head out with you?"

"Exactly."

Beatrice wiped her hands with the cloth. "You haven't killed me, so that's a point in your favor."

"I think we should leave now."

"Now? At this hour? Why?"

"I don't know. Just a feeling I have that these people will be closing in soon."

"Why would you think that?"

"They're very good at finding people. I know that from personal experience."

"I don't know how much more of this I can take."

Stone nodded, keeping his own counsel.

"When are we going to get out of here?"

"Maybe not today."

"Why not?"

"It's highly unlikely we will be able to paddle our way back to the mid-Keys or thereabouts, at least without getting spotted."

"So how are we going to get back?"

"I'm working on it. But right now we need to move."

"Now?"

Stone nodded. "We keep moving, we stay alive."

Seventeen

Catherine Hudson's cell phone vibrated on her bedside table, rousing her from a light sleep. She peered at the luminous text message from an old college friend, Becky McFarlane. The message read:

Hi, just saw your profile on LinkedIn and thought it would be nice to catch up sometime.

Hudson's foggy brain tried to process. She reread the short message two more times. She hadn't given out her cell number to anyone outside of work. She would have expected any contact to come through the LinkedIn messaging service, where her fake profile as a management consultant was public. The profile was to ensure her cover was in place across social media. But the approach had come via her cell phone.

Only a handful of people had that number.

Hudson felt something wasn't quite right. She hadn't seen Becky, a fellow economics graduate of Colby College, for almost twenty years. Her gut was telling her something was wrong.

She slipped out of bed so as not to disturb her husband and tiptoed downstairs. Hudson made herself a coffee. She opened up her MacBook on the kitchen table, logged on, and almost immediately pulled up Becky's LinkedIn profile. Her college friend, according to the profile, was working in consular affairs at the US embassy in London.

Hudson sipped some coffee and scrolled through the profile. She saw that Becky's previous employment was at the Bureau of Economic and Business Affairs in the State Department. Before that, she'd worked for the Diplomatic Security Service at the US embassy in Pakistan.

Alarm bells were beginning to ring. Big-time. Something felt wrong. Seriously wrong. Hudson knew the DSS wasn't only concerned with protecting diplomatic missions around the world. It was also involved in counterintelligence and counterterrorism.

Hudson had been recruited by the CIA straight out of Colby; the secrecy involved meant she had immediately lost touch with her college friends. She wondered why Becky suddenly wanted to get in touch.

If there was an ulterior reason for Becky's sudden approach, why now?

Catherine considered what she knew about the DSS. They were also involved in tracking down fugitives who had fled America to escape justice. In 1995, DSS special agents, along with local police and intelligence services in Pakistan, had arrested Ramzi Yousef, who had been wanted for the 1993 World Trade Center bombing. Diplomatic Security investigators had also been involved in a case involving a CIA station chief in Algeria, who eventually pled guilty to abusive sexual contact and unlawful use of cocaine.

She wondered if Becky worked in such a capacity. Then again, it might be something more mundane. But at the State Department, tasked with securing American interests and security, economic and political, around the globe, nothing was really mundane.

Of course, maybe a position in consular affairs was just a cover for more sensitive work. Hudson knew better than anyone that embassies were brilliant covers for intelligence-gathering operations. The CIA would have a presence, especially in a major world city like London.

Hudson took another sip of coffee as she stared at the pale-blue MacBook screen.

Hudson had always been taught that, in the world she inhabited, nothing was what it seemed. Friends could actually be enemies. Becky's LinkedIn profile was likely as full of bullshit as her own—Becky could be CIA, DSS, or something else entirely.

When Catherine thought back to their days at Colby, her lasting impression of Becky was that she was always the one who didn't want to go out, didn't want to socialize, didn't want to take part. She'd never initiated drinks, never suggested a double date. It just never happened with her.

But maybe she had changed after all these years.

Hudson figured she had four options. She could ignore the text. She could respond to the text and suggest they meet up sometime. She could respond to the text and say she wasn't available. Finally, she could call Becky and chat, without having any firm game plan in mind. Exchanging banalities. But then she thought, *That's exactly how it begins.* How to curry favor.

There was a possibility Becky was being used by others within US intelligence to reach out to her. Knowledge of her work, like most covert operations, was strictly confined to a handful of people. Few outside of that handful even knew about the Commission's existence, and none of them were supposed to know about her role in setting it up.

The CIA was very good at establishing privately funded entities to pursue their aims. A favorite tactic was sponsoring academic conferences that would attract, say, nuclear scientists from around the world. Invitations would be specifically extended to Iran's top experts on uranium enrichment. Then, covert CIA operatives would get to work, trying to approach the scientists without their Revolutionary Guard minders noticing.

Was Becky trying to set up something that was more than just a meeting of old friends? She imagined that Becky, working in the State Department, might be able to figure out what she really did. Maybe not the covert part, but she'd know Catherine was employed by the Agency.

A thousand thoughts were ricocheting through Catherine's mind as she contemplated what to do. The risk of making a wrong move was higher than ever, given the worsening Nathan Stone situation. If he, or the men hunting him, was ever traced back to the Agency, the fallout would be incalculable.

Just then her landline began to ring.

Great, she thought. *What now?* John's partner at the architectural firm would have called his cell phone. Her boss would have called hers. That left a family emergency—John's parents weren't in the best of health. She headed to the living room and picked up. "Yes?"

"Catherine? Oh my God, how are you? It's Becky McFarlane. I just sent you a text message, but I assumed . . ."

Hudson gathered her thoughts while Becky rambled on, her familiar voice taking Hudson back to dorm rooms and instant ramen and all-nighters before an exam. "Becky, you've got to be kidding me. What a lovely surprise. But it's the middle of the night."

"Oh my God, I'm sorry, I forgot. I'm so sorry. I'm in London."

Hudson's alarms were ringing at maximum volume. What the hell did she want? "Yeah, I just saw your message. How did you get my number?"

"I'm sorry I'm calling out of the blue. I can call back later if that's better."

Catherine noticed that Becky hadn't answered the question. "No, no, I'm wide awake. I can't believe I'm hearing from you after all this time. What a lovely surprise."

"How long has it been, Catherine? I don't even want to think."

"Two decades?"

"It can't be that long. Where has the time gone?"

Hudson's mind was racing. "Becky, I hope you don't mind me asking, but how did you get my number after all this time?"

"Your number? I called your husband. John. First time I've spoken to him."

Hudson was taken aback; she tried to compose herself. "I see. Sorry, I'm just a little surprised."

"It's my fault. You know what I'm like—so impulsive. He was on LinkedIn. I saw the number for his firm on his profile. So I called him."

"You called him? When?"

"A couple days ago, I think. He gave me your cell. And he gave me this number. And here we are!"

"Here we are indeed, how lovely." Hudson could barely contain her annoyance. "You should have just sent a message through LinkedIn."

"I wanted to hear your voice. I hope you don't mind."

"Not at all," Hudson lied.

"I was so excited to see your profile, you have no idea. So, you're a management consultant. That's really interesting."

Hudson closed her eyes briefly. "It has its moments."

"I can't believe you still sound the same. And your picture on LinkedIn, you look fantastic."

Hudson ignored Becky's attempt to ingratiate herself. "So, how's life treating you in London?"

"Busy. Crazy busy."

"I can imagine. Where are you working?"

"US embassy, processing passports. Pretty routine. Tell me more about your job. What does that entail?"

Hudson noted that Becky had volunteered the information about her job being *pretty routine*. "Advising firms on takeover strategies, outsourcing, that kind of thing."

"That is so amazing. What companies and sector?"

"Wide variety. Some technology, some hospitals—it's a pretty broad spectrum." Hudson allowed a silence to open up between them, compelling Becky to speak.

"Interesting. So, I was wondering—and I'm not going to keep you any longer with the time difference—if you might be free to meet up in a couple of days. I'll be back home in the States for my mother's birthday."

Hudson closed her eyes. She couldn't figure it out. She couldn't tell if Becky's intentions were legit. She wondered if she was overthinking a simple friendly call from a long-lost college friend. Then again, old friends who hadn't been in touch for years and suddenly reappeared were a red flag for any intelligence expert. "I'll have to check my calendar and get back to you."

"Yes, of course."

"But sure. I'd like that, Becky. I'm slammed with work at the moment, but by all means send me a message through LinkedIn. That would be best."

"Now that I've got your cell, I'll drop you a text. How about that?"

Hudson scrunched up her face, furious that John had given out her cell phone number. "LinkedIn messaging works best for me, if that's okay."

"Not a problem. If you insist."

"So tell me, are you married? Family?"

"I've had a couple of close calls, but no, nothing so far. To be fair, the amount of work I have, I struggle to look after myself without thinking about kids and a husband. Right?"

Hudson cleared her throat and forced a laugh. "So true. Look, great to talk to you, Becky. But I've got to catch an early flight. And I'm just about to hop into the shower. So, I have to run."

"Not a problem. Great talking to you again, Catherine. I'll be in touch."

"Please do." Hudson ended the call and let out a long sigh. Her heart was beating hard. She headed back to the kitchen and sat down at her computer. She was still mulling things over when her bleary-eyed husband walked into the room.

"Honey," he said, "who was that?"

"I'm sorry to wake you. It was an old college friend. Becky."

"What?"

"She said you spoke to her recently."

"Yeah, that's right. Sorry, I should have told you. Completely forgot."

Hudson looked at her disheveled husband and forced a smile. "That's okay, don't worry. It's not a big deal. Did she tell you what she wanted?"

"She's in London or something." John scratched his head and yawned. "Son of a bitch. I need more sleep, I'm telling you."

Hudson smiled. "Did she say anything else?"

"About what?"

Hudson shrugged.

"No, I don't think so. Just that she was going to be in town, wanted to meet up. I thought it was very thoughtful of her, to be honest. She sounded nice."

"She is. You've never met her?"

"Becky? No, I haven't. What's she like?"

"She's smart. Interesting. She's very pretty too."

John rubbed his face as if trying to wake up properly.

"I was just wondering . . ."

"Wondering . . ."

"Wondering why you gave her my cell number. It's not on my LinkedIn profile."

John shrugged. "Did she say that?"

Hudson wondered if he had just forgotten he'd told Becky her number. Her cell number was known, literally, to only a handful of people, and John knew how protective she was about maintaining it only for work calls.

"You sure you didn't inadvertently tell her your number?"

"How?" Hudson said. "She contacted my cell phone by text. That's the first contact I've had with her in twenty years."

John shook his head. "I don't get it."

"Did you maybe tell her the details? It's fine if you did."

"Absolutely not. I might have if she'd asked for them, but she didn't. I remember I had to volunteer the landline number."

"She didn't ask for my number?"

"Nope. I would've remembered that. Trust me."

Hudson smiled as her mind went into overdrive. Her husband's story wasn't aligned with what Becky had said. Either her husband was lying—but why?—or Becky had obtained her number by other means.

Something was definitely off.

Eighteen

Nathan and Beatrice made sure they left everything on the tiny island the way they had found it. They tidied up, blew out the citronella candles, which Nathan placed back in the cupboard, and removed the three bottles of water they still had left. It was important to leave as little trace as possible that anyone had been there.

They headed through the scrub and mangrove trees to the shoreline under the light of the moon.

Beatrice climbed into the boat. "Where are we headed?"

"Closer to civilization."

"Thank God. I don't know how much of this I can stand."

Stone pushed off with the paddle, Beatrice sitting at the front of the boat with her bag and the water. He paddled through the shallows into the darkness, occasionally letting the boat drift on the rippling current.

The sun would be up in a couple of hours. He couldn't afford to be complacent. The Commission would be redoubling their efforts now that more than twenty-four hours had passed. And he wanted to put even more distance between the trail they had taken after dumping the car and where they were now.

Stone dragged the paddle through the water, only a foot or so deep here. The moon was behind them, illuminating the channel's surface with a pale, ethereal glow. Lightning bugs and mosquitos filled the fetid air.

It felt good to be moving. They needed to keep moving. Vital. Stay still and they would die.

Beatrice turned and faced him as they headed east past the islands dotting the edge of the southern Everglades. "Are we gonna be okay?"

"We keep moving, we'll be fine."

Beatrice rifled in her side pocket. "Well, that's something."

"What?"

"I've got some Xanax after all."

"Good. Take it. Might chill you out."

Beatrice popped a couple of pills and washed them down with some of the water. She reached over and handed Stone the bottle. He took a gulp and handed it back to her.

"Let's conserve it," he said, and she nodded, then curled up on the floor of the boat. A few minutes later, she had fallen asleep.

When the sun peeked over the horizon a couple of hours later, washing that cotton-candy glow over the water, he turned and realized how far they'd come. They were two miles, maybe more, from the tiny island his friend had inhabited.

Gotta keep moving.

Stone paddled on. Through the seagrass and the twisted mangrove stumps, avoiding muddy sandbanks. Up ahead was a small island whose tiny sandy beach was shaded by mangroves and palm fronds on one side.

Stone jumped out and pulled the boat a couple of yards up the sand. Beatrice was still sleeping.

Stone left her like that while he got his bearings. He washed his hands in the water, then his face and his torso. The exertion of nonstop paddling had drained him. The heat and humidity were high already. He lay back on the sand and closed his eyes.

The sun was high in the sky—it was late morning perhaps—as he came to.

"Hey, you okay, pal?" a man's voice shouted.

Stone's blood ran cold. He sat up on the sand. Out on the water, twenty yards or so away, was a kayaker. Stone held up his hand and smiled. "I'm good. Just enjoying the Florida sunshine."

"How long you been out here?" the guy asked.

"Just a few hours."

Beatrice stirred and sat upright in the boat. She turned around and looked at Stone.

Stone wondered if she would say anything. He shielded his eyes against the fierce sun, stood, and moved close to her. "We don't know who that guy is," he whispered, "or who he's with. Just give him a nice wave. And say something sweet."

Beatrice looked over and waved at the kayaker. "Great day, isn't it?"

"You guys on holiday down here in the Keys?"

Beatrice spoke before Stone had the chance. "Just moving around, enjoying the sights and sounds of the Everglades."

"Looks like you've got some bad sunburn. You need some spray?"

Beatrice shook her head. "We're good. We're just headed off."

"Where to?" the guy asked.

Stone said, "Think we'll stop off on Cormorant Key."

"You got enough provisions?"

"We're fine, thanks."

The kayaker gave a wave of acknowledgment. "Well, you take care, guys," he said. "I'm headed all the way to the Flamingo Visitor Center."

"Good luck with that," Beatrice said.

The kayaker laughed. "I'm gonna need it. I'm about six miles from there." He paddled away, headed northwest, back to where they'd just been.

Stone waited until the guy was out of sight. "Well done. Smart response."

"You think he could've been one of them?"

"Don't know. How you feeling after your nap?"

"Dry. Hot. Feel like I'm burning alive."

"Lie in the water. That'll cool you down."

Stone knelt by the water, cupped his hands and dipped them, then splashed his face and hair. "See. It's good."

Beatrice gingerly stepped out of the boat, then hesitated. "I'm terrified of alligators."

"I think you're fine out here. A few miles back, it was thick with them. But I'd say we're fine."

Beatrice walked a foot or so into the channel. She knelt and lay back in the water, letting it soak into her hair and clothes. "That's better." She sat up and looked up at Stone. "We need to move, huh?"

Stone nodded. "Get back in and we'll try and put a few more miles between us and this place. The guy might inadvertently report this at the visitor center."

"You think so?"

"Sure. Might speak to a ranger at the center. And he might put out an alert. And that will attract the attention of the guys who are looking for us."

"What if you're wrong?"

"In what way?"

"What if the guys aren't interested in killing me? What if they're just interested in killing you?"

"You're within your rights to bail on me. But if I've learned anything over the years, it's that these people don't play games. They won't be able to sleep knowing that you might be out there, knowing what you know."

Beatrice stared out over the River of Grass and toward the islands in the distant haze. "This is crazy."

Stone shielded his eyes and squinted against the sun. "We need to move."

Beatrice got back in the boat.

Stone pushed off. "Keep your head down." He paddled relentlessly throughout the afternoon, ignoring the sun burning his back. Sunburn and heatstroke were risks he had to take.

He didn't rest until the sky began to darken.

Nineteen

Kevin de Boer's team was in one of three boats, which had fanned out through the southern Everglades. They had pinpointed the location of the original sighting by the conservation charity's cameras of Stone and the woman, close to the Snake Bight Trail. But their whereabouts at that moment were still a mystery.

"The fucker could be anywhere," he said to Bakker. "There are hundreds of goddamn islands where they could be hiding out. He could be on any one of them."

A voice in his Bluetooth headset. "Kevin," an analyst in Sarasota said, "we're just hearing from an old Seminole tracker who's with the second crew. There's a sign that they might've been on a tiny little key near Buoy Key, way out in Florida Bay."

"Copy that," he said. "Go ahead."

"The tracker and one of our team landed on the island to have a look. There are signs of an improvised shelter. Broken branches, palm fronds laid out. Cut quite recently."

De Boer adjusted his Bluetooth headset as he listened.

"We're looking at a map of the southern Everglades, Kevin. It appears that Stone had headed due south after going down the Snake Bight Trail. Then stole the boat and headed to the key."

"Then what?" de Boer said.

"If I was in his shoes, tell you where I'd go."

"Southeast?" de Boer asked.

"That would make sense. There are other islands where they could stop off."

"Then again, he might just decide to head north and back onto the mainland."

"More risky. Way more risky."

De Boer nodded. "So let's assume he does what we'd both do, head southeast. That means he's among countless tiny, uninhabited—perhaps uninhabitable—islands dotted across Florida Bay. Very difficult to track."

"But not impossible. We've already picked up his trail. He won't know that. He might suspect that we'll be after him. But he won't know for sure. Plus he's got the girl, who'll be desperate to escape."

"He might've killed her," de Boer said. "I'd be surprised if he hasn't already. He has to know she's worthless as leverage."

"It's a possibility. Probability I would say."

"So, if we both agree he'll head southeast, shouldn't we try and intercept him there?"

The analyst sighed. "I know the Keys real well. Grew up in Marathon. The coast guard patrols night and day around Islamorada for cocaine smugglers. If they catch our guys out there, they'll be wondering why a few of them were pulled over on the highway forty-eight hours earlier, and that would be a major red flag. Then we would be seriously fucked. The operation would be dead."

De Boer sighed and contemplated the best way forward. "I say we continue on. Let's spread out across Florida Bay. Let's try and use our technological advantages. We have our night vision. But let's listen in on the coast guard frequencies in case our guys are picked up."

"Got it."

"Another question is, What's Stone's plan going out there? Is he planning to hide out for a few days, weeks, and then head back to civilization?"

"Days would be far more realistic. He could survive out there for weeks, maybe months, by himself. But not with her."

De Boer ran a few scenarios through his head. "He'll head back to the mainland. And pretty soon. Cut and run."

"Yeah, I second that."

"This whole thing is fucked up," he said.

The analyst remained quiet.

De Boer felt empty as he stared over the dark waters. "He's already killed my brother. We've lost control of the situation. And it's very difficult to put the fucker back in the box."

"Huge area to cover."

De Boer sighed. "But not insurmountable. He's one step ahead, but not for long. Whatever it takes, this is one fucker we will put back in the box."

Twenty

In the far distance, Stone saw a speck of light on the dark water. He wondered if it was a boat. He paddled on, seagrass catching one wooden oar as it swept forward. He kept going for a few more minutes until he saw that the light was coming from an island up ahead. It was possible it was just some kayakers camping in the wild. He wondered if they should risk it.

Slowly, quietly, he paddled closer to the island.

"Do you think someone lives there?" Beatrice asked softly.

"I don't know."

He edged them closer. A glow emanated through the tangled mangroves.

Stone approached the island and jumped out into the seagrass surrounding the key. He dragged the boat through the reeds to a muddy beachhead that would conceal it from sight.

He headed deeper onto the island, followed closely by Beatrice.

"Are we okay to do this?" she asked.

"We'll be fine."

"What if we're not?"

"Jesus Christ, you're still alive. Why not hope for the best, huh?" Stone brushed through the mangroves toward the light. It was coming from a primitive wooden shack ten yards or so away.

The smell of a fire burning permeated the air. Food. He was ravenous.

"Hello, anyone home?" Stone shouted. "We got kinda lost out on the bay, hoping for a bit of shelter if possible."

In a rustle of wings, birds took flight across the Everglades sky.

Stone tried again. "Anyone home? Need some shelter for the night. Hope you don't mind us crashing in like this."

Still no answer.

Beatrice was standing beside him. "Someone's definitely around," she whispered.

"No question."

Beatrice cupped her hands and shouted, "Hello! Anyone here?" She swatted away some mosquitos. "Goddamn bugs. Eating me alive."

Stone cocked his head, and they moved toward the shack. He expected some kayakers to appear at any minute, as the smell of cooking got more distinct.

"No one here," she said. "How weird is that?"

Stone knocked on the rough wooden door and waited.

"Do you think this is smart?" she asked.

"I guess we'll find out soon enough."

Stone pushed open the door and looked inside. The ghostly glow he'd seen came from a paraffin lamp. A sturdy wooden table and chair and a single bed were the only furniture in the space. Maps covered the walls, and more maps lay on the chair beside a compass. Tidal charts. On another wall hung rifles, guns, machetes, knives, a crossbow, and arrows. The smell of burning meat was stronger now.

They stepped inside.

"Someone is living here," Beatrice said. "Where the hell is he?"

Stone's gaze was drawn to a door at the far end of the hut. He ambled over to it and pushed it open. It led to an open-air deck, built just a couple of feet above the water. He felt the platform moving to and fro with the ebb of the water.

At the far end of the deck, a pig was roasting over a spit, smoke and the smell of burning flesh filling the sticky air.

"What the fuck is this place?" Beatrice said.

It was clear the key was occupied. Had been, perhaps, for some time. Stone suspected the guy—and it would be a guy out here—was nearby. Maybe fishing. Getting fresh food to cook on his little island.

The more Stone thought about it, the more he wondered if they shouldn't just head off and find another island to wait out the night before they headed across to the mainland.

Beatrice swatted some mosquitos. "I don't like it here," she said.

"I was wondering if we shouldn't just move on to the next island."

Beatrice sighed. "This is creeping me out. Where is the guy?"

"He's out there somewhere. That's for sure."

"Do you think he built this place?"

"I don't know. Might've been built a long time ago. And someone has taken it over."

"This is the middle of nowhere."

Stone felt sweat running down his back.

"I don't like it here," Beatrice said. "I want to go."

A shot rang out, a shotgun shell whizzing past their heads.

Beatrice grabbed Nathan's arm and shrieked. He froze.

Out of the darkness emerged a silhouetted man on a boat, shotgun in hand. "Don't fucking move," he drawled.

Twenty-One

De Boer was in the lead boat as another followed, powerful lights fixed to their fronts, winding through the twisted mangroves that edged the shallow channel, checking for any signs of life.

He sensed they were closing in on Stone. What wasn't in dispute was that they were on his tail, perhaps closer than anyone imagined.

The boat edged around the far side of the island.

De Boer was with the old Seminole tracker as they headed to the north of the island. He disembarked with his team as they pushed through the mangroves on the island in the eerie darkness.

The team scrabbled through the undergrowth until they finally reached the center of the island. They came to a ramshackle wooden hut.

De Boer pushed open the door. Inside the hut was what looked like candle wax gathered in a metal bowl. He followed the tracker outside, who was on his hands and knees looking at a pile of leaves and twigs. The man carefully removed the covering, then whipped his head away. Piles of shit, flies and mosquitos eating it.

De Boer nodded. "Makeshift latrine."

The tracker looked inside and pulled out what looked like a tampon. He held it up.

"That is very interesting," de Boer said. "I'm guessing there aren't too many women out and about in uninhabited keys. I think we might assume that this is our actress."

De Boer turned to his team. "There's definite signs of life. Very recent. Within the last twenty-four hours maximum, And I would speculate that this is exactly where Nathan Stone and this young woman stopped off."

A voice in his earpiece.

"Kevin?" It was Bakker on the second boat.

De Boer relayed the find.

"I reckon," Bakker said, "he's going to be farther out, much farther out. And he's got the woman with him."

De Boer knew the guys on his team were loaded on amphetamines. It would help them keep going for days if need be. "They're out on one of the islands. I can feel it. Soon as we find them, it's kill on sight."

Twenty-Two

The burly man stepped off the airboat and onto the deck. His shotgun was still trained on Stone and Beatrice, who'd raised her hands. The man's face was burnished a blistered reddish brown from the sun, eyes the palest blue.

"You mind explaining what the hell you're doing?" the man asked.

Beatrice spoke first. "Sir, I'm really sorry, we're just kinda lost."

"Lost . . . You're damned right you're lost. What the hell do you think you're doing? You think it's acceptable to be on my property? Do you know I own this place?"

"We don't mean any harm, sir," she said, "I can assure you."

"So what the hell are you doing out here?" He stared at Stone. "Cat caught your tongue, son?"

Stone forced a smile as he kept his hands raised. "We had no idea anyone was on this particular island. If we'd known, we wouldn't have encroached on what's yours."

The man eyed them with suspicion.

Beatrice lowered her hands. "Could you not point the gun at me?" she said politely. "I have anxiety issues."

The man stared at her for what seemed like a lifetime before he burst out laughing. "Anxiety issues? You're not from Florida, are you?"

"No, sir, I'm from California."

"California. That explains just about everything."

Stone said, "Sir, we don't want to impose. But we were hoping to spend the night on your piece of land and then be on our way first thing in the morning."

The man looked long and hard at him. "Where you from?"

"I live most of the year in Florida," Stone said.

"I meant, what are you? Who do you represent?"

"What am I? Who do I represent? I'm sorry, I don't follow."

"I mean, son, are you from the government? Do you work for the government?"

"The government? No, I don't work for them."

The man didn't look convinced. "You people from the Feds?"

Beatrice smiled. "Hell no."

The man took a couple of steps forward. He peered at Stone. "You look military. You military?"

Stone took a moment to consider the best response and decided on truth. "I used to be in the army many years back."

The man stared at him for what seemed like an eternity. "Is that right?"

Stone nodded.

"Where did you serve?"

"Afghanistan. Iraq mostly."

The man sneered. "Fucking shitholes, right? What the fuck are we over there for? It's not our fight. Never was."

Stone said nothing.

"I don't like people turning up unannounced."

"Like I said, I'm sorry. Just looking for a place to rest up. I can see you're a man of honor. A man of principles. And I respect that."

"I know people who went to Iraq. Son went there. Didn't come back."

"Christ, I'm sorry. Truly."

"Just a fucking kid." The guy got quiet for a few moments. "You got lucky."

"Yes, sir, I did."

"I'm glad you made it back."

Stone nodded, sensing the man had made a connection with him. "I'm sorry about your son."

"Only a man who served his country knows what it's like."

"That's right."

The man pulled up the right sleeve of his shirt. His arm was tattooed with the word *Airborne.*

"The Screaming Eagles?" Stone said.

The man nodded. "The 101st. Fort Campbell. You know your stuff. I like that. I like that a lot. You're not some bullshitter."

Stone glanced at Beatrice before he fixed his gaze on the man again. "You mind putting the gun down? You okay with that?"

"You armed?"

Stone nodded. "Yes, sir."

"You know how this works, son. I can see you're not a novice. Very slowly gimme your gun."

"Just so there's no misunderstanding," Stone said, "how do you want me to work it?"

"Kneel down and slide it over toward me. Nice and fucking easy."

Stone did as he was told.

The man kicked the gun back along the deck behind him. "Now we're getting somewhere."

Stone got slowly to his feet.

The man looked at Beatrice. "Are you armed?"

"No, sir. I'm afraid of guns, actually. I'm nervous around them."

The man stared at her. "Yeah, figures."

"Please, you're scaring me," Beatrice said. "I promise I'm not a threat to you. I mean, do I even look like a threat?"

The man looked straight at Stone. "And what about you, son? Are you a threat to me?"

Stone shook his head. "We've been out on our boat for the last couple of days, and we just want to get back to civilization."

"So why don't you?"

Stone tipped his chin toward the water. "I think we started out in a certain direction, but I don't know . . . we just got kinda lost."

"You better not be the IRS. I fucking hate the IRS. Robbing bastards."

Beatrice smiled. "Trust me, we're not IRS."

"We just want to rest our heads for the night," Nathan added.

"If you could find it in your heart to let us stay, I, for one, would be eternally grateful. I'm not really an outdoorsy person, as you can see," Beatrice said.

The man looked at her long and hard. "You remind me of my wife in her younger days."

Beatrice flushed. Stone could feel her shaking a little.

"I didn't mean to frighten you. You understand why I have to be cautious?"

Beatrice nodded. "Perfectly understandable in the circumstances."

The man's eyes were hooded. "So, you got lost out here? I'm not sure I buy that."

Stone said nothing. He sensed the man could sniff out liars.

"Tell me the real story, son, or we're going to be having problems."

"Look . . . I want to be straight with you. It's a bit complicated."

"Your story's changing . . . It's complicated . . . How so?"

Stone sighed. "We're on the run. And we need to hide out."

The man kept his gun trained on Stone. "You're fleeing the law?"

Stone looked at Beatrice. "You want to explain to this gentleman?"

She winced. "Some people want him dead. And me too."

The man stared at her. "You shitting me?"

"It's not easy to explain."

"How did you meet him?"

"Long story. I was paid to chat him up at a bar in Miami and then get him to a party."

"A party . . ."

"I thought it was an audition. And I was paid. But it was just a ruse. I'm not making sense, am I?"

The man still had his finger on the trigger of his shotgun. His gaze fixed on Stone. "Why would they want you dead?"

Stone said, "Not sure you'd believe me if I told you."

"You wanna try me?"

Stone hesitated but realized he had no choice. The man wasn't going to entertain any more stalling or bullshitting. "A few years back—and this is classified; being an ex-military man, you'll know what I'm talking about—I worked sensitive jobs for the government."

"So, you *do* work for the government?"

"No. I used to in the past. I was contracted by the government."

"What kind of contracts?"

Stone said nothing.

"I'm waiting for an answer, son."

"They paid me money and I killed people. I was an assassin."

Beatrice closed her eyes. "This is a nightmare. Please don't talk about things like that."

The man said, "Why are you with him?"

Beatrice grimaced. "He told me that the people who hired me would kill me if I didn't tag along with him."

"What are you talking about?"

She explained in great detail exactly how she had been recruited for a fake audition and all the rest.

"That's a crazy fucking story."

Stone forced a smile. "We're not here to make trouble. We just want to hide out for a few hours. I suspect they'll have sent people to try and find us."

"You're damn right they will." He glanced at Beatrice. "Your friend's right. They will kill you."

The man lowered the shotgun. "I like people who speak the truth. Tell me more about these people who are wanting to kill you."

Stone said, "I think they're linked to the government. Hired by an organization that's used by the government."

"Our government? The American government?"

"Indirectly, yes."

"CIA?"

"Very probably linked in some way."

The man grinned, exposing stained teeth in the moonlight. He looked at Beatrice. "Why does that not surprise me? This country, we were born free. But somewhere along the line the government seems to have taken charge of everything. And I mean everything."

Stone nodded. "Are we good?"

"I believe so. Here's the deal: You play nice and don't try anything stupid, and you can hide out here overnight. You don't play straight— and let me tell you, and no bull—we got a problem. Are we clear?"

Stone nodded. "Absolutely crystal clear, sir."

The man stepped forward and shook Stone's hand. "Hunter Fredericks, pleased to meet you."

"Jimmy Ryan," he lied.

Fredericks stepped forward and shook Beatrice's hand. "And you're an actress?"

Beatrice blinked away the tears and nodded as if in shock.

"I never meant to fire my weapon like that. Just had it as a precaution. Force of habit. It's the South, we look after ourselves."

"I understand."

The man showed them back into the hut. "Not much, grant you, but it's all I've got. And for tonight it's yours."

Beatrice swatted away a mosquito. "How do you live out here? This is crazy."

"I fought in Vietnam. That was crazy, let me tell you. This? Piece of cake. You just gotta toughen up. Gotta be resilient."

Beatrice put her hands on her hips and shook her head. "I don't know. I'm freaking out with all the wildlife. And the dark. I don't like it."

"Grew up not far from here. This doesn't scare me. This environment protects me. It's nature's shield. Speaking of which, I caught some beautiful fish. I'm going to cook 'em up with the roast pig. How does that sound?"

Beatrice looked at Stone, who nodded and smiled encouragingly. "Sounds great."

Fredericks was as good as his word. He fed them and allowed them to use the rudimentary shower he had constructed. Then he opened up an eighteen-year-old bottle of single malt. He handed them chipped mugs and poured in the liquor.

He raised his mug. "To your good health and this wonderful country!"

Stone knocked backed his drink. The Scotch warmed his guts. It felt good.

Beatrice winced as she swigged hers. "Jesus, that was nice," she said.

Fredericks looked pleased. "It is, isn't it?" He filled up their mugs again. He took a gulp and sighed as his gaze wandered between them. "Helluva way to get to know people," he said.

Beatrice smiled. "I'm very grateful for your hospitality out here, let me tell you."

"We're fellow Americans. We look after each other, right? That's the rules."

Stone nodded. "You mind me asking how you ended up out here?" he asked.

"I wanted to disappear. Just like you."

"What from?"

"My tow-truck business failed. Wife left me. I was broke. About to be homeless. A broke veteran. So far, so predictable."

Beatrice said, "What about your kids? Couldn't you have lived with them?"

"I didn't want to impose. I was embarrassed. Besides, I had to serve time for an IRS problem that sort of snowballed. Filing false accounts or some such bullshit. You believe that?"

Beatrice nodded empathetically. "I know all about the IRS. Pain in the butt."

"Ain't that the truth," he said.

The conversation flowed for over an hour. Fredericks talked about his marriage, his ungrateful children, and all manner of gripes. He talked of isolation, talked about feeling adrift from twenty-first-century America. But mostly he raged about all the sins he thought were afflicting the country. The work-shy, the blacks, the spics, Antifa fruitcakes, leftists, liberals, gays . . .

Fredericks stared into his chipped cup. "I don't know what the fuck we've become. Who are we? Are we as a species going to survive for another hundred years, let alone a thousand? I doubt it. I'm supposed to care about these fucks? Degenerates the lot of them."

Eventually, Beatrice began to yawn and stretch. "Interesting," she said, noticeably uncomfortable with the tone and the subject of conversation. "I'm beat. You mind if I call it a night?"

Fredericks looked up at her with heavy eyes. "Not at all, young lady. You need your beauty sleep, right?"

Beatrice smiled, looking uncomfortable. "Indeed."

A short while later Stone called it a night too. He and Beatrice were sleeping on mats on opposite sides of the wooden floor in the main room.

"I'll keep watch," Fredericks said. "You guys look dead beat."

Twenty-Three

Despite Fredericks's offer to keep watch, Stone slept lightly, so he was instantly alert to movement in the darkness. He stayed perfectly still. The creaking of wooden floorboards was followed by a startled murmur. Then a man's voice, hushed and threatening.

Stone turned his head slightly and peered across the room. Bathed in shafts of pale moonlight, Fredericks's hulking frame was on top of Beatrice, his hand over her mouth.

Stone held his breath, letting his eyes adjust to the dark. He could see that Fredericks's other hand was pinning Beatrice's right arm to the floor.

Stone turned gently onto his side, facing away from Fredericks. Fredericks still had his Glock—Stone had seen him lock it in a gun cabinet. It wasn't a smart choice of weapon in this situation anyway—any struggle on Beatrice's part meant there was a chance he'd hit her instead of Fredericks. But he'd chosen the mat on this side of the room for a reason. Glistening on the wall next to him was Fredericks's array of weapons, including a serrated steel dagger. A hunter's knife. He stretched up until he was able to lift it from its hook and gripped it tight.

Stone turned over again as quietly as he could. The wooden floorboards creaked.

Fredericks whipped his head around. The whites of Beatrice's eyes shone in the moonlight. "What the—"

Stone got up and rushed him. He grabbed Fredericks by the hair and stabbed him hard in the neck. Blood spurted from veins and arteries. Down and down he thrust the knife repeatedly into Fredericks's neck.

Beatrice screamed and curled into a ball.

Stone hauled Fredericks's huge weight off her and flung him onto the floor. The bastard was gargling blood as he lay dying.

"What the fuck were you playing at?" Stone roared.

Fredericks gasped for breath and began to groan. "Please . . . please."

Stone bent down and plunged the knife into his chest. When he stepped away, Beatrice released a high-pitched scream.

Stone hauled her to her feet. "It's over, do you hear me?"

Beatrice was shaking, pulling down her top. "The dirty bastard!"

"It's over."

"He tried to rape me!"

She looked down and saw the blood pooling around Stone's feet. Her hand flew to her mouth. "Oh my God. He's dead."

"I know."

She punched Stone in the arm. "What the hell did you do that for?"

"You just said he tried to rape you!"

"You killed him. You fucking killed him."

Stone grabbed her by the shoulders. "Of course I had to kill him. What do you think he was going to do to you?"

"You're fucking crazy!"

"Maybe. But you're alive, aren't you?"

"I'm alive. But I'm standing next to a killer."

"I know what I am, you don't have to remind me. Should I have just let him rape you? He would've killed you afterward. And then me. Do you think he would have allowed us to leave here afterward?"

Beatrice went quiet.

"Well, do you?"

"Probably not."

"You're fucking right. He would've killed us and thrown us in the water to be eaten by crocs or gators." Stone took his hands off her. "Now pull yourself together and—"

Beatrice hugged herself tight. "I hate it here!" she screamed. "Do you hear me? I hate it! This is like a living fucking nightmare."

"We're going to get out of here."

"I want to go home."

"You will."

"You said that before."

"In good time. Soon. But we need to be smart. We need to focus."

She was breathing too fast, beginning to hyperventilate. "What in God's name have we done?"

Stone grabbed her by the shoulders. "Listen to me. In situations like this, you either kill or get killed. The guy was a predator. And trust me, he wasn't going to take no for an answer."

She nodded, her breaths still coming rapidly.

"You need to breathe slowly. Slowly . . . Take your time."

Beatrice closed her eyes and did as she was told.

"That's right, good. Slow it all the way down . . ."

In a minute, her breathing was back under control. Beatrice began to pace the room.

"Okay?" Stone asked.

She nodded.

"Just breathe."

"I'm fine," she snapped.

Stone held up his hands. "Just relax. We're getting out of here in two minutes. Do you want to sit out on the deck while I deal with the body?"

Beatrice's eyes widened. "What does that mean?"

"What do you think it means?"

"How the hell would I know? Unlike some people, I don't make a habit of racking up dead bodies."

"Well," Stone said dryly, "then now is as good a time as any to learn that there are no good options for disposal. We could leave him here. The flies, insects, and some wildlife would peck away at him."

"That's disgusting."

"We could take him with us."

"Not an option."

"Or we could throw him overboard in a deeper channel of water and allow the crocs—"

"You're going to feed him to the crocs?"

"Do you have a better suggestion?"

Beatrice sighed and shook her head.

"Okay, how about I get him on the boat and dump him? Then I come back for you."

"You're not leaving me here by myself. I'm coming with you."

Stone nodded. "Fine." He gathered up the guns, knives, military crossbow, machetes, all the weapons off the wall, then the flares, $5,000 in cash, and placed them in a backpack. "You wanna help?"

"Sure."

"Get the maps, water, and whatever food he's got. I'll get this fuck into his boat—we'll make better time with it, and we'll leave the other boat here."

Beatrice stared at him as if in a trance.

"I'm really sorry that happened. But we need to get going. So, we need to pull ourselves together. Can you do that?"

Beatrice nodded and began to move.

Stone dragged Fredericks's hulking body by the feet through the hut and out onto the deck. He rolled the bloodied corpse onto the airboat.

A minute or so later, Beatrice emerged with the backpack containing the handguns and knives, two plastic bags with cookies, potato chips, bottles of Coke and water, insect repellent. And a bag holding rifles and ammo.

Stone and Beatrice took one last look around before they stepped onto the airboat. He started up the motor and checked the GPS display.

"He's still bleeding out," she said.

"Don't look at him."

Beatrice turned and looked out over the dark waters.

Stone inched the airboat away from the makeshift jetty and gently negotiated the low-lying sandbanks. When they'd reached deeper waters away from the island, he turned off the engine.

Beatrice was hugging herself tightly as Stone rolled the body off the boat and into the water. It quickly sank out of sight.

Stone waited for a few moments as he got his bearings.

"What about his children?" Beatrice said quietly. "What if someone misses him?"

"You can never tell anyone about this. You want to go to trial in Florida? Trying to explain how he was going to rape you? The press would have a field day. And the public? Not the most forgiving, let me tell you, no matter the circumstances."

"What if the body resurfaces?" she asked.

"It will."

"What?"

"Eventually, it will bloat with water and float to the surface. But it'll also be unrecognizable. The crocs and gators and God knows what else will have torn most of the distinguishing features off of it."

Beatrice went quiet as Stone restarted the engine. "This is insanity. Complete insanity. None of this is real. It can't be."

"It's real." Stone stared out over the brackish waters. "And now we need to move on."

"When is this nightmare going to end?! I just want it to end!"

"It will end. But we need to stick together and not panic. The moment we begin to panic, we're dead."

Twenty-Four

Just before dawn, Berenger's cell phone rang.

"Mark?" It was the gruff voice of Kevin de Boer.

"Yeah, go ahead."

"Turn on your TV. Switch to channel 528."

Berenger picked up his remote control and pressed the keys. The screen showed real-time night-vision footage from the Everglades of what looked like the inside of a log cabin.

"You got it?"

"Got it. Where is this?"

"Three nautical miles from the last key they visited. You're seeing what we're seeing. We have a team that just disembarked onto the island."

"Is this someone's home?"

"We believe so. We don't know who. But there are clear signs of life there. But also this . . ."

The camera panned to what looked like stains on the floor.

"This is blood. We're going to take samples and test the DNA to see if this is our guy. Or maybe the person who lived there."

Berenger stared long and hard at the congealed blood. "You think this might be Stone's blood? Or the girl's?"

"We don't know."

"Take a guess. What do you think happened?"

De Boer was silent for a beat. "There are signs of long-term habitation on this key. So the question is, Where is the person who hangs out there? My guess? My best guess? Stone arrived there, things didn't work out with him and the guy living there, and Stone killed him."

"Why?"

"No idea. Take your pick."

"Any estimate of how long the blood has been there?"

"That's a tough one."

"Guess."

"A matter of hours. Might've happened five, six, seven hours ago."

"Kevin, this is your area of expertise. I'm deferring to what you know. Could he have killed the girl there?"

"It's a possibility. So is an accident."

"You don't believe either of those scenarios?"

"You can never be entirely sure. But I think Stone killed whoever was living there and grabbed the provisions. Shelves are pretty empty. Guy has to be a survivalist type to live out there."

"What about the girl?"

"What about her?"

Berenger sighed. "I mean, where the hell is she?"

"She's with Stone. That's what I think."

"Against her will?"

"Maybe."

"You think she might've gone willingly? Why the hell is she still with him if not under duress?"

"It doesn't really matter. She's with him. I'm convinced of it."

"Get your guy to show me the rest of what's in and around this place."

The night-vision footage roamed through the wooden hut. Two mats laid out for sleeping, one bed. A wall full of empty hooks. Pots and pans. On the deck was a half-eaten pig on a spit.

"Who the fuck lived out there, Kevin?"

"Like I said, survivalist probably. Screwball. Who knows. But whoever it is, is gone."

"Are we sure he's not nearby out hunting or something?"

"We've scoured nearby. Nothing."

Berenger put himself in Stone's mind-set. It should have been easy to do, given how well he knew him. But then again, Stone had already surprised him by not killing the girl. Something was going on that Berenger couldn't put his finger on. Stone couldn't have changed so much in the year since his raid on the Commission. Could it have something to do with the actress's resemblance to his sister? The idea gave Berenger a little thrill—in a way he felt as though he were still pulling Stone's strings. "There are hundreds of other islands around Florida Bay and beyond, right?"

"I've been told the Keys occupy nearly a thousand square miles. A lot of space to hide in that."

"Every hour we don't get him is an hour he's closer to disappearing for good."

"We're closing in," de Boer said confidently. "But we need to get lucky to find them out there."

"I don't want to hear about luck. We need to change our fucking luck, Kevin. I want that fucker. I want the woman. And I want them both dead. Before they make it out of the Everglades."

Twenty-Five

A tangerine dawn peeked across the horizon, bathing the water in an eerie pale-orange glow. Beatrice was curled up in a ball on the wooden floor of the airboat. He wasn't sure if she was actually asleep.

Stone felt exhaustion wash over him. The events of the early hours had taken their toll. Beatrice had finally been starting to trust him. Now he worried that she might try and disappear, endangering herself and him in the process. If she did, he couldn't blame her. She was so far out of her comfort zone it had to be traumatizing for her.

Stone checked the GPS and saw they were within a mile of Cluett Key. It was an east-west tide as they approached the island through seagrass-filled water, the spray on his face. He switched off the engine and jumped out. He was knee-deep in mud, silt, and sand as he hauled the boat ashore, up past the mud bank, up the beach and beyond the high-tide mark. "You wanna shake a leg?" he said. "Need some help."

Beatrice stirred and handed him the backpack containing the weapons and flares, the plastic bags holding the food, and the bag containing the guns and ammo. She jumped off the boat and immersed herself in the warm water for a few moments.

"Feeling better?"

Beatrice shook her head. "What do you think?"

Stone turned and led the way farther inland. They headed through some cypress and marshy grasses and into a clearing. He took a machete out of the backpack and began to chop down branches for a makeshift shelter. "Keep busy. It'll help."

Beatrice sighed. She held up the wooden frame as he tied the pieces together with vines, layering palm fronds on the base. She swatted away a cloud of mosquitos. "Goddamn fucking insects!" She pulled out the insect repellent and sprayed it all over herself. "I'm being eaten alive. Fuck!"

Stone carefully laid down more palm fronds. "Be careful with the sand flies," he said.

"What?"

"Be careful. They'll be burrowing away just beneath the surface. The females will feed on your blood."

"I need to get out of here."

"Let's get the shelter up, get a fire going, get some breakfast, and then we can talk."

Beatrice grumbled for a while but reluctantly unpacked the provisions and placed them neatly on the fronds.

"Keep the flares away from the fire, for God's sake," he said.

"Do you think I'm stupid?" she said.

"No, I don't. Just being cautious."

"Cautious?" She swatted away a cloud of mosquitos. "This is terrible. I can't put up with this any longer, I'm telling you." She lashed out at some bugs. "Fuck!"

Stone tried to ignore her. He cut down strips of black mangrove wood and threw them on the fire. They gave off a pungent aroma, almost like incense.

"What is that? It stinks."

Stone hunched over the fire. "It's supposed to. The Native Americans and early white settlers who lived out here used this to get rid of mosquitos and bugs."

Beatrice scrunched up her face, unimpressed.

"Swamp angels, they used to call mosquitos."

"How do you know this stuff?"

"Long story."

"I want to believe that you can get us out of here. I'm trusting you."

Stone nodded his head. "I know you are. And I want to get back home just as much as you do."

Beatrice closed her eyes as she sat on the sand beside the makeshift shelter.

The sun was rising, and the acrid black smoke was dissipating in the breeze.

"Won't this give away where we are?"

"It might. But in an area so huge, unless you're in a plane going overhead, you won't spot it. More importantly, it stops crocs and snakes from getting near you. Besides, kayakers, day-trippers, and survivalist crazies like Fredericks all have fires on beaches and islands all over Florida Bay, or didn't you notice?"

"I noticed all right. I'm not stupid, you know."

"Never said you were."

"We're in the middle of nowhere and I feel like I can't breathe. We're so isolated. I don't like isolation. Never have."

"Not as isolated as you think."

"What do you mean?"

"Think about it. Fredericks. Kayakers. Wildlife students. All hanging around. It's not the raw wilderness it was a thousand years ago."

Beatrice heated up some canned beans and spaghetti, which they ate from the pot. "I feel like I've been out here for a lifetime."

Stone smiled. "You're killing me with your whining, do you know that?"

"Don't even joke about killing." It was her turn to smile.

"Feeling better?" Stone said.

"Marginally," she said.

Stone could see she was once again putting on a brave face. It didn't take a genius to recognize that she was scared witless after Fredericks attacked her, more aware than ever that she was out in the wild with a strange man.

Stone fixed his gaze on her. Tears streaked her dirty face. Blood from mosquito bites dotted her arms and neck. "If it means anything," he said, "I'm sorry for dragging you all the way out here. I'm sorry for all the shit that's happened."

Beatrice closed her eyes and began to cry. "I need to get out of here. I'm truly losing any grip I once had on my sanity."

Stone picked up Fredericks's map of Florida Bay and began to examine it. He used a compass to gauge their position and which direction they needed to head. He flattened out the map across the fronds and pointed to their location. "We're here. Cluett Key."

"Okay, what are our options?"

"I'm guessing from this map—and it's very rough—that we've traveled just over ten miles."

"Is that all?"

"Most of that was paddling. But Fredericks's boat has a motor. There's a rudimentary GPS on board, but it works. That's good. We have a map and compass. That's also good."

She looked at the map. "We're going to die. Or if not, they're going to kill us."

"Not necessarily. We need to focus. And not freak out. You got that?"

Beatrice hugged herself tight. "I don't know."

"What do you mean, you don't know?"

"I mean, I feel sick, I'm scared, I'm lonely, and I'm totally not dealing with this."

"Well, you better. And quick."

Beatrice nodded. "Easier said than done."

"Here's how I see it. We could either go due east, and we reach Tavernier."

"Where's that?"

"Close to Key Largo, Upper Florida Keys. I know a guy who runs crab boats out of there. But that means going through all this mangrove, seagrass bullshit. We could easily run aground in this boat. It's different from a kayak or a canoe."

"Due east is the closest to civilization?"

"That's correct. Unless we head back the way we came, and that's not an option. So, while going east to Tavernier is an option, the quickest way would be due south to Layton."

"So Layton it is?"

"No, that's not my favorite option."

"It isn't? Fuck, why don't you ever make things easy? To me, we head due south and we're home and dry."

"That's what they'll be thinking too."

"Who?"

"The people who want to kill us."

Beatrice blew out a frustrated breath. "So, what do you propose?"

Stone pointed toward Cudjoe Key on the map. "I know this place. I know a guy who lives near there."

"And?"

"And he'll help us. He'll pick us up."

"That's assuming we get there."

Stone nodded. "You're right. It's not a slam dunk. And it's a long, long way from here."

"How far?"

"I estimate . . . it won't be much short of sixty miles."

"Are you fucking kidding me? In that airboat? A fucking airboat!"

"Yes."

"This is getting crazier and crazier."

"By heading to Cudjoe, we will, I believe, stay clear of not only the people who are trying to kill us but also the coast guard. That route gives us the best chance."

Beatrice bowed her head and began to sob again. "Sixty fucking miles. I just want to go home. I don't care if the coast guard finds me. I want them to."

"Well, I don't. So we stick to my plan. There are two main coast guard stations in the Keys. Islamorada and Key West. So, we need to be south of Islamorada."

"I don't know. I just want to get out of here."

"You're not fucking listening. We need to focus. Are you alive right now?"

Beatrice closed her eyes and nodded. "Barely."

"You're alive. But we need to think strategically. We need to avoid two groups of people. Those fuckers who want to kill us, and the government forces who are up and down these waters all the time. What is so difficult to understand about that?"

Beatrice said nothing as she swatted some bugs from her face.

"Once we're on the Keys, we'll be fine. But until then, you need to trust me."

Beatrice sighed long and hard. "So when do you envision us heading out of here? I'm exhausted."

"So am I. We both need to be alert. So, I think the best course of action is to rest until dark."

"We wait for night?"

Stone nodded. "The boat has GPS, so we're good to travel at night. Fredericks knew his stuff, sick bastard. We head off and stick to a steady thirty, we should be there in a couple hours."

"Tonight?"

"Yeah, that's the plan. We've got a full moon. With no cloud cover, we'll be fine."

"I don't know," she said.

"What don't you know?"

Beatrice shook her head. "I just have this vision of us getting hit by a coast guard boat, some bigger boats, you know."

"It's a risk."

"Why don't we just leave now?"

"Why? Well, if we pull up on Cudjoe Key in broad daylight, there's a very good chance we'll be spotted."

"Spotted by who?"

"Anyone. I want to get ashore without anyone seeing us. So my friend can pick us up and get us to safety. Besides, there's a sheriff and a deputy or two on Cudjoe. So night would be best to arrive. Think about it."

"Think about what? I just want to get the fuck out of here!"

"So do I. But there are ways of doing things. If we get picked up by the cops, they'll start asking us questions. They'll want to know if we stole the boat. Is the airboat ours? If so, where's proof? You see where I'm going with that? There will be ramifications."

Beatrice got quiet.

"What are we going to say? *Yeah, we stole it off some survivalist nut, and then we killed the fucker?*"

"Are you kidding me? *We* didn't kill the fucker. You did."

"He was trying to rape you."

"*I* didn't kill him. Listen, I want to go now. Right fucking now!"

"Does that sound like the plan? I don't think so. It sounds like a surefire way to get arrested."

"I want to go now!"

"Not an option."

Beatrice glared at him, arms folded. "So, I'm a prisoner?"

"You're getting emotional."

"Why, because I'm a woman?"

Stone shook his head. "Don't twist my words. I just meant you're not thinking logically. And yes, you're getting emotional."

"You're damn right I'm getting emotional. Why the fuck shouldn't I be getting emotional? Yes, I am emotional. Tired. Exhausted. Close to the end of my rope. Do you understand, you crazy fuck?"

Stone sat and said nothing.

"No, I don't suppose you do understand this."

"I want us both to get back to civilization in one piece, and that means not getting arrested and not letting some local take video of us stepping off the airboat and upload the footage to YouTube. In my line of work, that wouldn't be good."

"Your line of work? You don't have a line of work. You're a fucking assassin. You maniac."

"Look, you just need to be a little more patient."

"Patient? For what? So some fucking snakes or crocs can eat us? I am fucking dying here!" Beatrice lay down on top of the palm fronds, curled up in a fetal position, and began to sob.

Beatrice cried her heart out. Eventually, her crying subsided and she fell into a deep sleep. Once he was sure she wouldn't wake up frightened to find herself alone, Stone left to cut down more fronds to block the shafts of hot sunlight burning down onto the sleeping actress. He put out the fire with some sand, then headed through the mangroves to the muddy beach. He used a stripped piece of bark to check how much gas was in the airboat tank. It was low. He filled it up from a rusting metal canister Fredericks kept on the boat.

Then he pulled the boat farther up the beach and covered it with palm fronds until it was concealed from scrutiny.

Stone headed through the mangroves fringing the island and back to the clearing. He looked inside the makeshift shelter. Beatrice was still sound asleep. The noise of gulls punctuated the susurration of the waves lapping onto the key. The smell of burning black mangrove still hung in the salty air.

He watched her for a few minutes. She looked peaceful. Serene even. She was showing greater resilience than he had expected. Sure, she was griping. Moaning. Bitching. But she was hanging in there. He admired that.

Stone's mind flashed to the South Beach bar. He remembered her face that night. There had been something slightly mysterious about her independent of her resemblance to his sister. She'd seemed strangely confident. It could have been that she'd popped a couple of Xanax and drunk a couple of shots before she walked into the bar. Picturing the scene made him think about the others in the bar.

Had the Commission been watching him for a while? A day or two perhaps?

It wasn't a stretch to think that they'd caught him visiting his sister, despite the pains he'd taken to slip into the facility unseen. But he could also imagine that facial recognition software had pulled up his new face. The whole of South Beach was awash in surveillance cameras for businesses, bars, public buildings, you name it. Maybe the cops in Miami Beach had spotted him. Was the cop who'd been hanging around the Deuce every night feeding the Commission information?

The more he thought about it, the more he wondered if that was how it had happened. He would probably never get to the bottom of how they'd found him. The chain of events.

Stone gave himself a shake. He'd been standing there with his eyes closed. He needed sleep. Badly. He crawled into the shelter and lay down on the fronds, his back to Beatrice, as exhaustion overcame him.

Twenty-Six

The office of William Black, the Director of the CIA's National Clandestine Service, was on the seventh floor of the George Bush Center for Intelligence. Catherine Hudson was escorted from a security checkpoint in the lobby up to his office. He stood staring out of the window, cell phone pressed to his ear. He turned around and motioned for her to take a seat.

Hudson sat as the door quietly shut behind her. She looked around the office; this was the first time she'd been there. On the wall hung two black-and-white pictures taken in the wake of 9/11. The one on the left showed the smoldering ruins of the Twin Towers; the other showed the terrible damage to the Pentagon.

She shifted in her seat.

Two phones occupied Black's desk. One provided an internal secure line to any CIA station in the world.

"I want it in forty-eight hours, son—those figures are crucial before we green-light this."

Black ended the call and sat behind his desk. "Catherine, do you ever sleep?"

Hudson forced a smile. "That bad, huh?"

"No, I don't mean that. I mean you work like I used to work ten years ago. And it takes its toll, let me tell you."

"I'm okay, really."

Black nodded as he leaned back in his leather seat. "Haven't seen you around for a while."

"You know how it is, sir. No need to be here."

"How are you finding working out of that satellite office? Does it suit you?"

"It suits me fine. It's just that . . ."

"Home life?"

Hudson forced a smile. "Yeah, home life. How did you guess?"

"Everyone who works at the Agency has home life issues. Believe me, I know. I was the same. It puts a strain on things. But . . . we go on."

Hudson took a few moments to compose herself. She would have preferred to talk about the Commission. But Black had an innate ability to know when one of his charges was having issues.

She looked at him. Ice-blue eyes, perfect knot in his tie, starched white shirt, navy single-breasted suit. His gaze often unnerved people, almost like he was trying to figure out what was ailing them. As if he had to know what mental shape they were in.

Hudson knew a lot of CIA operators who felt uneasy in his presence. She had never felt like that. Not even once. She had worked for Black since he was the station chief in Kabul. She'd watched the way he negotiated the byzantine relationships with visiting State Department dignitaries, tribal leaders, Pentagon wonks, politicians wanting a photo opportunity. He was impeccably polite, cordial; he exuded warmth. But Hudson knew that he was old-school. He was tough as teak. He would not allow insubordination. He didn't mind a frank exchange of views, but once the course or direction had been set, it was a foolish man or woman who tried to change his mind.

Black looked at her long and hard. "Catherine, we've known each other a long time, right? I know it can't be easy having to keep up appearances over the years. I'm talking about your official cover as a management consultant."

Hudson nodded. She wondered how he knew or sensed that things weren't good at home.

"I know better than anyone the tensions in a relationship because of the hours."

"Sir, I'm not here to talk about my private life. My private life is just that. Private. And I'd appreciate if we didn't focus on that area. I'm here to talk about the project. My project."

Black sighed. "Lot to talk about."

Hudson nodded.

"So, what are we going to do about it?"

Hudson had been thinking of nothing else since Stone had gone on the run. "When the Commission was set up, you said I was responsible."

"Go on."

"And that the only person I should speak about it with was you."

"That's correct."

"You also said that you wanted to be kept abreast of progress or otherwise. If things were going wrong."

Black leaned back in his seat. "I asked you a question. What are you going to do about it?"

"You need to know—and I'm not going to sugarcoat it, sir, you know how I operate—that I believe the Commission has gone off the rails."

"Its implementation has not been without setbacks, I grant you."

"Sir, I am seriously concerned. What started off as a carefully modulated, unacknowledged special-access program has become a living nightmare."

Black said nothing.

"That's how I see it."

"I'm not disagreeing."

"I believe some of its objectives were realized, but the potential fallout is catastrophic."

Black's eyes fixed on her. "Have you ever wondered why I gave the go-ahead for the Commission?"

The defense of America. The defense of the West. The defense of our values. And Black had always stressed that the fight must not be in America's own backyard but thousands of miles away from home. He was a reactionary. A realist.

"I think I remember, sir—correct me if I'm wrong—that you said that it would be an invaluable way to achieve American objectives by proxy."

Black nodded. "Without risking direct responsibility."

"I believe this element now means that my vision for the organization has run its course."

"Catherine, I know your family well."

"Indeed, sir."

"Your grandfather, Henry Hudson, was my mentor."

Hudson shifted in her seat. "I didn't know that, sir."

"A long time ago. You know what his legacy is?"

Hudson said nothing.

"You've probably heard of the Safari Club."

Hudson nodded.

"Your grandfather was, as you know, a great man and a brilliant patriot. He was one of those who worked with our overseas intelligence partners to set up the program."

Hudson cleared her throat. She knew all about the Safari Club. But she didn't want to say any more than she had to.

"He had a great way of looking at things from a fresh angle. Some would say from out of left field. I would describe it as resourceful. Innovative. A bit like yourself."

Hudson shifted in her seat.

"He was ahead of his time. Always was. But the Agency was on the defensive in the midseventies after Watergate and all that bullshit. You know how he found a way around the new restrictions?"

Hudson smiled.

"Way back in 1976, the intelligence agencies of Egypt, Iran, Saudi Arabia, and France began an informal arrangement—which we were party to, although we didn't admit it at the time—to share information in a bid to thwart the spread of communism and Soviet influence. The reason this was set up was because—"

"We were hamstrung after the Church Committee report, I believe."

Black grinned. "That's exactly right. But your grandfather, he had the foresight to realize that America couldn't just allow the Russians to shape the world. We had to be in there fighting our corner for our friends and allies."

"What's your point, sir?"

"My point is, the Safari Club was a brilliant idea whose time had come. The Commission is another."

"Sir, the Commission, after recent events, might very well result in blowback for the Agency and potentially even the country. We've contained the wild-card threat Stone represented until now. But I believe the time has come for the Commission to be wound up."

Black smiled. "I love that you still care so much, Catherine."

"Sir, my analysis shows the returns are vastly outweighed by the risks. Look at the resources the Commission is expending to kill one of their own. This isn't furthering America's interests; it's distracting from them. We have to shut it down."

Black took a moment before he answered. "I hear what you're saying. It's good to care about our work. That's such an admirable trait. By the time you get to be my age, cynicism and paranoia are the order of the day. With you? I see optimism. Hope. I really like that about you. Which makes me wonder why you're proposing ending the Commission."

"Events have overtaken us. I think it's plain to see that. We should have pulled the plug after Stone went rogue in Scotland."

"He killed the target first—Senator Crichton. That was the plan, right?"

"Perhaps, but that should have been a warning. I couldn't understand for the life of me why Clayton Wilson, who'd had such an illustrious career at the Agency, would allow Stone to be hired for a second job after that."

"Hindsight's a lovely thing. The kidnapping of Stone's sister should have worked."

"The operative word being *should*. The fact of the matter is that Stone should never have been allowed that second opportunity. It was a flawed assessment. And the rest is history. Something I'll have to live with. Clayton Wilson did not understand the full extent of the threat he unleashed by bringing Stone back into the fold."

Black shifted in his seat. "You're casting aspersions on late Director Wilson, one of our most esteemed intelligence experts since the Second World War."

"I know, sir. And his loss is a tragedy. But how many more are we willing to lose? How public are we willing to let these embarrassing mistakes become? The failure to neutralize Nathan Stone in Miami is unforgivable, and every hour he's on the loose brings a greater chance that taking him out will involve public attention we won't be able to cover up."

Black was silent for a few moments, reflecting on what she'd said. "What's the latest intel on Stone and the girl?"

"They're somewhere in the Everglades, perhaps in or around Florida Bay."

"Can't they call in the coast guard?"

"They could. But they don't think that's a wise containment strategy. Neither do I."

"I believe we have a new operations director."

"De Boer."

"Which one?"

"Kevin."

"I know Kevin well. He's very thorough. Methodical almost. He'll find him."

"Sir, I believe there comes a time to consider cutting our losses. I believe that time has now come."

"Catherine, you know how many plausible-deniability operations I've been involved in?"

Hudson shrugged. "Quite a few, I'd imagine."

"That's right. And there wasn't one that didn't involve some previously unforeseen shit hitting the fan at one time or another. The key is not to throw out the brilliant idea but to persevere. It's important to press on."

"But sir, with respect, what if this isn't closed down, Nathan Stone is not neutralized, and this all gets out? What about the Agency's reputation?"

Black grinned. "If it gets out? Nothing to do with us. It's just some retired, right-wing CIA crazies."

"Sir, I'm not sure that will hold up to intense scrutiny."

Black shrugged. "Maybe . . . Catherine, only Mark Mahoney was sniffing around all this. He was eventually taken care of. All the documentation on encrypted files was bleached."

"There will be others. Nathan Stone knows so much it's worrying. There's another matter I'd like to raise with you."

"Sure. What's the problem?"

"Out of the blue, an old college friend of mine has gotten in touch. I haven't heard from her for at least twenty years."

"What's her name?"

"Becky McFarlane."

"Name doesn't ring a bell. What's the problem?"

"Sir, I sense that she was making an approach with ulterior motives. She used to work at the State Department. Now she works out of the embassy in London."

Black allowed a silence to stretch between them. "You think this Becky is fishing for information or intel?"

"I don't know. I don't like it."

"I'll check it out. Fingers crossed it's nothing. Just an old friend wanting to say hello."

"Maybe. My main priority, though, is Stone and this goddamn actress. It's a grave situation. But I remain convinced that we need to shut down the Commission, from top to bottom."

"Look, I'll tell you what I'll do. I hear what you're saying. But I think we can make a decision after Stone and this woman are dealt with."

"What if they're not?"

Black smiled benevolently. "That's your job, Catherine. To ensure they don't make it out of the Everglades alive."

Twenty-Seven

Stone felt himself drifting on a sea of darkness. Floating on the tide. Darkness all around. Then the sound of a faraway explosion. Bright-red fireworks.

He felt cold metal pressed to his head and bolted upright, wide awake.

Beatrice was staring down at him, gun pressed to his forehead. The sky was lit up by a red flare, burning brightly.

"What the hell?" he said.

Beatrice took a step back. "I want the keys."

Stone stared at the sky, which had illuminated everything for miles around. He got to his feet. "Are you fucking insane?"

"Gimme the keys to the boat!"

Stone stared at her in disbelief. "Do you know what you've done? Do you have any idea what you are doing?"

"I'm getting out of here. Now! Gimme the fucking keys!"

"You have just alerted *them* and the coast guard and every boat in and around Florida Bay that there is an emergency. It means they know where we are. They will find us. Do you realize that?"

"I want someone to rescue me!"

"Really? I thought I explained the situation."

"That's your situation. Your reality. Things have changed. I want out. Right fucking now."

"You're not thinking straight."

"Why? Because I'm a woman? Is that it?"

"That's not it. You're not thinking straight because you're scared."

"I've got a right to be scared. I'm fucking petrified."

"I understand that. But this is not how we get out of this situation." Stone got to his feet. "Gimme the gun."

"Not a fucking move, psycho."

Stone looked at the sky all around him. It was just a matter of time before they'd be found. "We need to get out of here. They could be here any minute."

"I'm going. Without you. Hand over the keys or you're going to be sorry."

Stone took a step forward and shook his head. "I can help you get out of here. To safety. But we need to move right now."

"I'm at the end of my rope. I'm finished. You're shooting people. That survivalist tried to rape me. Enough! Anything has got to be better than this!"

"I thought you trusted me."

"So did I."

"I can get us out of here."

"I'm going alone."

"I can't allow that."

"What do you mean, you can't allow that? What does that mean?"

Stone slammed his fist against one of the shelter's poles. "What you did was insane! You let your emotions override your critical-thinking faculties. And now you've endangered both of us."

Beatrice gritted her teeth, tears in her eyes. "I want to live! I don't trust you!"

"I haven't harmed you. Not once! I will not harm you. Didn't I say I would protect you and get us to safety?"

Beatrice said nothing, gun trained on his face.

"I will not break my promise to you. I will guide us to safety. You need to trust me."

"Why the hell should I trust you?"

Stone sighed impatiently. He grabbed her wrist and sharply twisted her arm, prying the gun out of her hand. He pressed the gun to her head. "See how easy it is to lose that advantage?"

"You bastard!"

"Grab our bags and get in the airboat right fucking now!"

"You're a bastard. A cold, unfeeling bastard."

"Get the bags and get in the fucking boat."

Beatrice snatched up the bags of food and water. "You son of a bitch."

Stone grabbed the backpack containing handguns and knives. He herded her through the mangroves back to the airboat. Once the boat was on the water, he climbed in. "I can't believe you did that. Crazy bitch."

"I can't stand this anymore! Don't you get it?"

Stone sighed.

Beatrice looked at him, tears in her eyes. "Look, I'm sorry. I panicked. I don't know. I'm freaking out. I'm human."

"Let's focus. And let's get out of here. How does that sound?"

"Do you forgive me?"

"Don't let it happen again. Lie down so you're out of sight."

Beatrice complied. "Where are we going?"

"Change of plan." Stone turned the key in the ignition. The engine spluttered but didn't start. He tried it again and again. Nothing. "Are you kidding me?"

Stone waited a minute before he tried it again. The engine creaked and clicked. But still it didn't come to life.

"Tell me it's not broken."

"Quiet!"

Stone tried three more times. The engine didn't even make a sound.

"It's dead?" she said. "The goddamn engine is dead?"

"And we will be too if we don't get this into gear." He tried the engine once more. This time it spluttered and groaned and fired up. "Thank you!"

"Thank you, Lord!" she said, looking up at the crimson sky.

Stone flicked on the GPS. He scanned the six-inch plastic monitor showing his position and the best route to take. "Yeah, so we're going with plan B."

"What do you mean?"

"I mean my original plan will have to be shelved, at least for now."

"What the hell?"

"If we're going to the mainland, we won't be able to outrun them in this thing, not after that flare lit up the sky."

"So what are we going to do?"

Stone edged the airboat away from the shore and pointed it southwest. "You'll see."

Twenty-Eight

De Boer was in the lead boat snaking through Florida Bay toward the position of the flare, approximately eight miles away. He radioed Bakker. "You got any further details?"

"Latitude 25.0304 degrees north. Longitude 80.8645 degrees west."

De Boer checked a map with his flashlight. "Cluett Key. ETA four minutes. Let's approach from the northeast."

The sky was a dark red, caused by the illumination from the flare. He wondered what had happened. He knew Stone wouldn't have set off the flare. Which meant—if it was indeed them—that the woman was responsible. Maybe Stone had abandoned her. Maybe she'd seen her chance to escape. Maybe it was an accident.

"Let's do this right, people," de Boer said to the three others in the boat. "I don't want us running aground. I don't want us chasing shadows. Let's focus. We find them. And we kill them."

Bakker called in. "ETA two minutes, thirty seconds."

De Boer pulled back the slide of his gun. Closer and closer the boats advanced toward the island. "Now listen, we don't know who sent up the flare," de Boer said. "It might be a kayaker. Might be a frat boy partying with some friends. Might be a coast guard exercise. So let's be wary."

"You know as well as I do this is them," Bakker said, the excitement in his voice unmistakable even over the radio. "Of that I have no doubt. This is Stone and that fucking actress."

"I agree," de Boer said. "But let's keep switched on. Let's not get complacent."

"We've been focused. And we're going to finally put this bastard to bed for a long sleep."

De Boer cleared his throat. "It might be a fucking trap."

"Wouldn't put it past Stone. He's dangerous."

De Boer stared at the island as the boats skimmed the water. "ETA?"

"One minute and fifteen seconds," Bakker said.

"Copy that," de Boer said. "First things first. The woman. Be nice. Get her out of there if she's alone. Persuade her to get onto the boat."

"Then?"

"Then kill her."

"What about Stone?"

"Kill him and bury him on the island. This ends now."

Twenty-Nine

Stone hit the gas on the airboat as it skimmed across the grasses and shallow water. The salty spray stung his burnt face and arms. "You okay down there?" he shouted to Beatrice.

"I'm fine. No . . . I'm not fucking fine. I'm an idiot. Shit, I'm sorry."

"Let's deal with the situation we're in now and not dwell on the past. We need to put some water between us and those guys."

"How do you know they'll be following us?"

"As sure as night follows days. Trust me. I know these people. I know their next move."

"What does that mean?"

"It means I try to imagine what they would do. And as soon as that goddamn flare went up, they were alerted."

"Not necessarily."

"I know they're nearby. You need to assume they're on your tail and you'll soon be dead. You need to have that edge."

"Don't say that. You're scaring me. There's no evidence the people who want to kill you are following us."

"I don't need evidence. What I know about them indicates that they will be nearby. Very nearby. Far closer than we imagine. And that's why I'm taking such precautions. That flare likely brought them right to us."

"Don't say that. I'm frightened as it is."

Stone peered out into the darkness ahead, then glanced at the GPS. He turned around but didn't see anything apart from the pale-red glow still lingering from the flare that had gone off a few minutes earlier.

"Are we going to go to the mainland? Please tell me we're going straight to the mainland."

"No can do. Not just now."

"Why the hell not?"

"Because if I know the people looking for us, they will be very well equipped, with fast boats and God knows what else. They'll catch us easily and kill us. We need to be smart."

"How the hell do we do that?"

Stone said, "Just keep your head down." He took his foot off the gas. The airboat began to slow. He checked the GPS, then negotiated some low-lying sandbanks.

"What the hell is going on?"

"I need to make sure we don't run aground."

Stone edged through a narrow stretch of shallow water until he got back in the direction he needed to be going. He opened up the gas, and they sped off through the River of Grass, the pale moon casting its ghostly glow over the dark waters. Up ahead was the silhouette of an island.

The GPS indicated they had reached Dead Terrapin Key, south of Whipray Basin. He jumped out and sank into the muddy silt. He had to haul himself out of it. Then he pulled the airboat up through mangroves and onto a sandy beach. Beatrice jumped out once they were on the beach, carrying the backpack, the bag with guns and ammo, and the plastic bags.

Stone dragged the airboat higher on the shore. He looked around, establishing a line of sight and getting his bearings.

"Why are we stopping here?" she said. "This doesn't make any sense!"

Stone motioned for her to lie down beside the line of mangroves that ringed the island. "Flat down!"

"What is it?"

Stone peered into the distance. "Fuck."

"What is it? Tell me!"

"They've spotted us."

Far out on the wetlands, maybe a couple of miles in the distance, he saw what looked like two boats. And they were headed straight for them.

Thirty

Berenger was pacing the control room in the underground facility in Sarasota. He was beginning to feel the pressure gnawing away at him. His stomach ulcer was burning. He popped a couple of Zantac. A few minutes later the symptoms subsided, and he glugged a can of Coke. The huge screens on the wall displayed real-time footage as the two boats approached a small island on Florida Bay. The thermal imaging picked out the ghostly white figures of de Boer's men, crouched in the boat, as they got closer to the dark island.

He crossed the room, transfixed by the events on the screens. De Boer was wearing a Bluetooth headset, on the lead boat communicating with Sarasota and the second boat.

Berenger watched with a sense of trepidation. He knew what Stone was capable of. And what he might do when cornered. The thought chilled him to the bone. But now it seemed like time was finally running out for Stone and the down-on-her-luck actress.

He sensed they were nearing the endgame.

The boats were around twenty yards or so from the shoreline. Berenger stared up at the screens. On the periphery of the scene, he thought he saw something: two ghostly figures running into the mangroves and out of sight.

The voice of de Boer. "We got a visual."

Berenger's heart began to race faster.

De Boer said, "Nice and easy, people. My team will approach from the northwest. Boat two, go ashore where you are. Let's squeeze those fuckers."

"Copy that."

The footage showed one boat edging closer to the beach.

Berenger closed his eyes and smiled.

Thirty-One

Stone crouched low as he smeared mud all over his face, arms, and neck and did the same to Beatrice.

"What the hell are you doing?" she asked.

"I'm trying to minimize the chances of thermal-imaging cameras picking us out."

"Does it work?"

"It's not foolproof. But if our clothes are wet, it might fool the technology for a few minutes."

Stone noticed that the two boats were still approaching. "Fuck!" he said.

Beatrice was lying on her stomach beside him on the sand, the mangroves providing cover. "What do we do?" she whispered. "They're coming from both sides."

Stone saw that the boat on the northwest side of the island was about twenty yards offshore, edging slowly toward them. He saw the silhouettes of four men on board. Their chances of overcoming four operatives were not great. "Gimme the backpack." She handed it to him and he pulled it onto his back. "Head down. We're going to crawl back the way we came. Do you understand?"

Beatrice didn't respond; she seemed to be in shock.

"Do you understand?"

"Yes," she whispered.

Stone began to crawl across the sand, through the stand of mangroves. Beatrice was right behind him. He caught sight of a boat with one man in it, driven partially up the beach. He took off the backpack, reached in. He felt Beatrice virtually on top of him. "You need to keep down."

"My God," she whispered, "who's that?"

"It's one of *them*. The people I was telling you about."

"They're going to kill us?"

"That's their plan." He handed her a 9mm Beretta, pulled back the slide, and flicked off the safety. "This is locked and loaded. Only pull the trigger if this guy gets me or if I say so. If he gets me, take the fucker out. Then get in his boat and get out of here."

Beatrice took the gun.

"Do not point it at me, do you hear?"

She was shaking, huddled beside him. "I got it."

Stone reached into the backpack and pulled out the military crossbow. He looked through the sights at the silhouetted figure who had jumped out of the boat.

"What are you going to do?"

"Quiet," he said.

Stone held his breath as he lined up the target. He focused. And waited. And waited. Then he squeezed the trigger.

The bolt hit the man square in the chest, and he collapsed onto the sand.

Beatrice gasped.

Stone felt adrenaline surge through his body. He got up and hauled Beatrice with him as they dashed down the beach toward the high-powered airboat. He picked her up and virtually threw her into the boat, along with the backpack and bags. Then he hauled himself on board. He started up the engine and headed out of the shallows, careful not to stall the engine.

He switched on the GPS and saw their position east of the island. He maneuvered the boat slowly around the northern tip and then headed out half a mile into the channel and cut the engine.

The boat drifted.

"What are you doing?" she whispered.

"Be quiet."

Stone took out the rifle and locked the magazine into place. Lined up the sights. Crouched low. He saw four figures on the beach through the crosshairs, their boat unattended.

He got the fuel tank in the crosshairs.

"Wish me luck," he said.

"Oh my God . . ."

Stone held his breath and pulled the trigger three times. The bullets ripped into the gas tank, blowing the boat to pieces in a fireball explosion.

"What the fuck have you done?" Beatrice shrieked as the sky lit up around them.

Stone started up the engine and they sped south, away from the men. Shots whizzed over their heads.

"Stay down!" he shouted.

Beatrice peered over the bow of the boat.

"I said get down!"

Suddenly a bullet whizzed by.

"Aren't you listening? Get the fuck d—"

Before he could get the word out, Beatrice let out a piercing scream and clutched her shoulder.

Thirty-Two

Catherine Hudson stared in horror as the real-time feed of a fireball in the Everglades lit up the screen in her Arlington office. She felt as if she were going to be sick. She kicked over a trash can. "What the fuck is going on?"

She began to pace up and down the office, seething at the sequence of events that had spiraled out of control.

Hudson fumed as she tried to gather her thoughts. She wondered who she should call first. She sent a text to Black, updating him and asking to speak immediately. A few moments later her cell phone rang.

"Catherine, is this secure?" It was Black.

"Yes, sir. Secure line." She succinctly explained what had just happened out in the wilds of the Everglades.

Black sighed. "I don't get it."

"I'm looking at the footage right now; the sky is lit up like a bomb went off. I wouldn't be surprised if they can see it in the Keys."

"Are you kidding me? They had him surrounded? Shouldn't they just have shot up Stone's boat? He couldn't have gotten far after that."

Hudson felt sick. "I don't think they'd located the boat yet. I believe they were eager to get onto the island and shut it down really quick."

"Eager to get onto the island? I can't believe we've gotten to this stage. This was all about self-containment, plausible deniability. We had no fingerprints. An explosion means the coast guard and the local police. It means explanations will have to be provided. God knows where it'll end."

"Sir, that's exactly what I was trying to tell you. We need to shut this operation down."

"Okay, we are where we are. I assumed with de Boer and his guys on it, this was a slam dunk. Turns out I was wrong." Black was quiet for a few seconds. Then he swore. "What's so difficult about wiping this fucker out?"

"Stone is resourceful. Smart. We trained him, after all."

Black was silent.

She wondered if her comment had come across as a rebuke, so she pivoted. "The question is, Where do we go from here, sir? Doing nothing is not an option."

"What we don't do is interfere with the work of de Boer, Berenger, and the Commission."

Hudson sighed, frustrated. They had to do something.

"There must be no trace of our involvement," he said. "That was what we agreed when the Commission was green-lighted."

"Sir . . . I have to disagree. Say he gets to shore, sir. And hands himself in. Says he's Nathan Stone. And tells the full story of what he knows about the Commission. What the hell happens then?"

Black sighed. "I'm going to have a stroke with this bullshit."

"Sir, I'd like to make a suggestion."

"Yeah, go ahead."

"No direct interference. Agreed. Also, let's leave aside any talk of dismantling the Commission for the time being." She knew she wasn't going to get any traction there, so why waste her breath? "What I propose is a shadow operation."

"By us?"

"By contractors, not us. You know the guys I'm talking about?"

"Yeah, they're very good . . . Interesting."

"It's paramount, of course, that this is off the books. The budget might be tricky."

"Leave that to me. We've got numerous ways of doing sensitive jobs."

"I propose that I lead this. I created this. I will resolve it."

"I can't put anything in writing."

Hudson knew what that meant. It meant that if there was blowback, she alone would take the fall. A rogue midlevel CIA operative. And those at the highest levels of the Agency would be protected. "I'm aware of the implications, sir."

"Are you?"

"Absolutely, sir. I know how it works."

"You will be putting yourself at risk, hypothetically, if things go to shit."

"Once we don't take risks, we're not doing our job. I remember you said that at a seminar once."

Black sighed. "Your grandfather was the same way. He was all for blurring boundaries."

"Then it's only fitting. Leave it to me. I'll put in the calls."

Thirty-Three

Stone turned off the engine and let the airboat drift while Beatrice screamed incessantly in pain. He took off his soaking shirt and ripped it into strips.

"Motherfucker!" she yelled, gritting her teeth.

Stone kneeled down beside her. He touched the wound and felt the warm blood on his hands. "You were lucky."

Beatrice was arching her back, eyes shut tight. "What? Are you kidding me?"

"An inch to the right and the bullet would've ripped through a major artery."

Her skin was cold to the touch. It wasn't good. But Stone couldn't tell her how bad it was.

He wrapped the shirt strips tight around her upper arm to stop her from bleeding out. He pulled the ends as tight as he could.

"Fuck!" she yelled. "You bastard!"

Stone knotted the strips even tighter. "We need to stop the bleeding."

Beatrice began panting as the pain and shock really kicked in.

Stone held her hand. "I will get you help. I will not leave you. I promise."

"I need to go to a hospital. Fuck."

"Leave it to me. I know a doctor."

"What? I want to go to a hospital, motherfucker!"

"No can do," Stone said.

Beatrice cried in pain. "What? Please . . . I don't want to die!"

"You go to a hospital, they will find you. And then kill you."

"Have you lost your mind? I need hospital treatment. I need to see a surgeon. I need civilization!"

"If you go to a hospital, two things will happen. First, they will get the bullet fragments out of your shoulder and save your life."

"That's a good thing! Thank the Lord."

"But second, *they* will know where you are. And you will be neutralized in the blink of an eye. Your name will register on the hospital computer. And they will be watching for things like that. Do you understand?"

Beatrice was breathing hard. "I'm bleeding out."

"I know you are. I will get you help. Trust me. Do you trust me?"

Beatrice fell silent and closed her eyes. She was losing consciousness. Fast.

Stone scrambled across the boat, back to his seat, and started up the engine. He hit the gas pedal. He set the course for an isolated area of the Lower Keys.

The airboat sped across the water as Stone prayed he could get Beatrice to dry land before it was too late.

Thirty-Four

De Boer cradled Bakker, crossbow bolt in his chest. His gut felt empty. He had lost Pieter, the younger brother he had always looked out for. Now Kevin had lost Bakker, one of his oldest friends. They'd grown up together in rural South Africa. Farm boys.

He, and only he, was responsible for both their deaths. He could have tasked someone else with the missions. Pieter didn't have to go out on the motorcycle. And Bakker should have stayed with him on the lead boat. What the hell had he been thinking? Now he had lost both of them. A brother, his flesh and blood, and his closest friend. And for what? For a mission that was doomed from the get-go.

De Boer cradled his friend as the other operators crowded around on the beach, feeling himself being engulfed by a raw fury. He was in charge of this whole fuck-up.

He felt an arm around his shoulder as one of his team consoled him. "Kevin, I don't know what to say."

De Boer took a few moments to compose himself. He imagined his father in Pretoria, his reaction when he heard the news. He wouldn't say much, if anything, but then would retire to his room. Alone. To grieve. That was how his father would deal with it. He would retreat into his shell, not wanting the world to see his pain. Then he thought about his mother. She would be crushed to know that her beloved youngest son had died in some fucked-up operation that wasn't even his fight. He imagined that his parents would be better able to deal with it if Pieter had died serving their country. But he hadn't. He'd died as a mercenary. For money. Nothing more, nothing less.

And now Roel Bakker. One of the good guys.

Fuck. In the name of God, why? And for what?

He began to push those thoughts to one side, as he had been trained to do. He had the rest of his life to grieve. Besides, Pieter and Roel had to be avenged. Pure and simple.

De Boer carefully extricated himself from cradling Roel and signaled everyone to gather in front of him. He looked around at the faces of the tough operatives who were left. "We've got a job to do. We need to focus and do it. Pieter and Roel are no longer with us. God bless them. My brother, however, was not the sort to countenance any sentimentality. To him, it was all about the here and now. So the operation goes on. Am I making myself crystal fucking clear?" Nods all around. "Can you hear me, Sarasota?"

The voice of the computer whiz. "We hear you, sir."

"Stone and the woman, son. They were both there. The flare went off! We should have had them. So, where are they now?"

The computer whiz said, "I have night-vision footage from a long-range drone up on one of the screens."

"And?"

"It took longer than expected to get this operational," the computer guy said, "but it is what it is."

De Boer nodded. "How long has it been active?"

"It left the airfield in Miami four minutes ago. Fixed wing. Range of three hundred miles. Full capabilities. We'll find them."

De Boer knew using the fixed-wing drone was his last option. It would be picked up by radar; he knew that. But as long as they kept away from military facilities and civilian airports, they would hopefully be fine. He thought of his brother again. Roel lay with a blanket over him, waiting to be evacuated by a backup team. Kevin felt as if his heart had been ripped out. His soul. He felt like breaking down. But he didn't.

De Boer stared at the sky and looked around. The Everglades. The islands. The water. The thick, ancient, forested wilderness.

The computer guy said, "We're going to have the drone fly to Cormorant Key and head south from there. It's equipped with heat sensors and advanced facial recognition software. I swear to God we will find them, Kevin."

"Height?" de Boer asked.

"It's flying at ten thousand feet, so they won't even know it when we do find them."

De Boer's cell phone rang.

It was Berenger. "Kevin."

"Sir . . ."

"Christ, this is terrible. I want to express my deepest condolences to you once again."

De Boer sighed, never feeling more alone. "I appreciate that, sir."

"It might seem like the wrong time to raise this, but I'm going to raise it anyway."

"Sir?"

"Both Pieter's and Roel's wives and family will be well looked after. Financially, I mean."

De Boer didn't know what to say. He had just lost his brother and his best friend. But he felt compelled not to tell Berenger to go to hell.

"Anyway, I'm really sorry for your loss."

"Shit way to go. But . . . we all know how it works."

A long sigh. "Kevin, if you want off this job, I'll understand. I want you to know that I value your expertise and I believe you should have the time and space to grieve in peace. This is too much for one man."

"Not an option, sir," de Boer said. "I'm not walking away from the job that cost Pieter his life. And Roel. I'm going to see this through. I'm going to find Stone and the woman. And they're going to pay for this if it's the last thing I do."

Thirty-Five

Stone pushed the airboat to the max, the saltwater spray drenching him, while Beatrice lay motionless. She hadn't moved for nearly a minute. He negotiated the choppier seas away from the mangroves and seagrass. In the distance, maybe a mile or so away, he saw lights. He slowed down. Then he took his foot off the gas.

He glanced at the GPS, then peered through the darkness. Up ahead was what looked like a bay boat, used in shallower waters to fish. As the bay boat drew closer, Nathan took out the 9mm from his waistband and placed it at his feet.

Aboard the boat were two big-looking guys, each with a can of beer in their hand. The boat's powerful searchlight nearly blinded Stone.

"You okay, brother?" one of the men shouted across to Stone as they slowed down.

"I'm fine, man."

"What the hell you doing out here?"

Stone realized the guys were blind drunk. "I was about to ask you guys the same."

"Just some fishing. Came up from Cudjoe. Making a night of it. You want a drink?"

"No time, thanks."

The younger of the two peered into the airboat. "Hey, who's that? Is that a chick? Is she okay?"

Stone shook his head. "Shoulder was bleeding out, so I'm taking her back to dry land. Really need to step on it."

"What the hell happened?"

Stone knew he couldn't say she had been shot or they would think he did it. "Diabetic. Collapsed and lost blood as she fell onto the rocks."

"Holy shit," one of the guys said.

"Gotta get a move on, you see."

"Sure, man. You want us to escort you back?"

"Much appreciated, guys, but I got this."

The older man said, "You want me to call for help?"

"Already did," he lied. "Really need to get going. Hospital is waiting. I think it's superficial. Once she gets the insulin and they clean the wound, she'll be fine."

"She's out of it, man," the younger one said. "You need to get her to the hospital real fucking quick."

The older man picked up the radio. "I'll get on the hailing channel. Coast guard will be here in no time."

Stone restarted the engine and gave a good-natured salute. "No need to confuse them, already done that. They're meeting me a few miles south of here."

"Oh I see. Are you sure?"

"Absolutely. They've got a medical guy on board too, so she'll get help real quick, don't worry. But I appreciate the concern." Stone edged the boat forward. "Enjoy your fishing, guys. I need to get her to the doctors and they can patch her up good."

"Sorry for holding you up, man," the older guy said.

Stone smiled and got back on course heading southwest, away from the fishermen. He felt the tension dissipate the farther away he got. Mile after mile. But all the while Beatrice didn't move.

Thirty-Six

It was the dead of night and Berenger, unable to sleep, was sitting in his upstairs bedroom in a mansion on a Florida island, watching footage captured by the drone as it swooped through the Everglades.

His cell phone rang.

"Mark?" The gruff voice belonged to Fisk, the man who bankrolled the Commission. "Seems like Nathan Stone isn't giving up without a fight."

Berenger sighed. "We're on it. And we'll get him."

"I'm not sure it'll be that easy."

"The drone allows us to track him. He's ours."

"Mark, I'm getting worried. I'm not a natural worrier. But this is not fucking good for my blood pressure. We're making mistakes. One after the other."

"Stone's luck is about to change."

Fisk sighed. "I hope so. Any sign of him so far?"

"Negative. But we will get him, make no mistake."

"Mark, I keep hearing the same thing."

"Sir, to be fair, this was badly conceived from the word *go*. That's why it's such a disaster. That doesn't mean we won't get him. He will make a mistake."

"So when's the breakthrough?"

"Sir, we're on it. We've run into a few problems, I admit, some of our own making, some deriving from Stone's ingenuity. But we caught a break with that flare."

"Let's cut the bull. Nathan Stone is outsmarting us. At every turn."

"The drone will make the difference, of that I've been assured."

"Assurances don't mean shit, Mark. Why wasn't the drone deployed earlier?"

Berenger rubbed his eyes. "We considered it, but de Boer thought it was better to use the operatives on the ground. He was concerned the drone would register on radar stations and people would start asking questions."

"And have they?"

"Nothing so far. But the drone ownership traces back to a shell company in the Caymans, so there isn't anyone to question about it anyway."

"What if they shoot it down?"

"That's not going to happen. The US Army is allowed to shoot down consumer drones, but only if they're buzzing their facilities. So, it's basically illegal to fly a basic-model drone within four hundred feet of a US Army base. But what we're operating is a far larger long-range drone, or unmanned aerial vehicle, as the army likes to call them. They're subject to the rules for manned aircraft."

"So as long as we steer clear of federal airspace and passenger plane traffic, we'll be fine?"

"Absolutely." Berenger stared at the drone footage on his TV. Suddenly, up on the screen a tiny speck appeared in the sea.

"Are you still there?" Fisk asked.

"Yes, sir. Bear with me . . . I'm just going to put you on hold for one minute." The onboard camera zoomed in fast on the airboat skimming across the water. It was clear as day: there was a woman lying flat on the bottom of the boat and a man driving.

The earpiece crackled into life. "Mark, it's Kevin. Are you watching? That's them."

"Copy that."

The camera zoomed in closer. Berenger could see the familiar features of Nathan Stone's reconstructed face.

"Son of a bitch," Berenger said.

"That's him, isn't it?" de Boer said.

"You better believe it. What's his location?"

"Six miles northeast of Marathon."

"Fuck. He's going to make it ashore."

"But not for long."

"Don't lose him this time. I want all resources deployed. He must be neutralized."

Berenger ended the call. His heart was beating hard. He picked up his cell phone and relayed the information to Fisk.

"That's what I want to hear, Berenger. That's more like it. The next time we talk, I want to hear that the fucker is dead."

Thirty-Seven

It was late and dark as Stone steered the airboat toward Sombrero Beach, Marathon, in the middle of the Florida Keys.

He took his foot off the gas as they got nearer. He let the boat's momentum take it a hundred yards closer. Then he cut the engine as the waves lifted the boat up onto the beach.

Stone jumped out and lifted Beatrice out of the airboat, before slinging her over his shoulder. He took her farther up the beach and laid her gently down in the sand. He retrieved the bags with the weapons from the boat and kneeled at her side.

"Hey, man," a voice said.

Stone turned and saw a kid ambling toward him smoking a joint.

"What happened to the girl? She looks out of it."

"She's a bit more than out of it. She was injured out on one of the Keys. Need to get her to the hospital. You got a phone?"

The kid stared down at Beatrice as if his brain was struggling to process Stone's question. "Sure thing, bro," he said. The kid pulled an iPhone out of his pocket and handed it over. "What the hell happened?"

"Long story," Stone said, taking the cell. "We need to get her help."

"She's bleeding out onto the beach, man. Fuck."

"Can you do me a favor?" Stone said.

"Yeah, of course, man."

"Can you watch her for a minute while I make the call?"

"Sure, whatever. She's not going to die, is she?"

"Just watch her."

Stone headed farther along the beach, out of earshot. He punched in the number of an old friend. The call was answered on the fifth ring.

"Yeah, who the fuck is calling at this time of night?" Stone was relieved to hear the voice of Barney McKeever, a vet who'd been a medic in Vietnam.

"Barney, it's Nathan."

A long silence.

"Yeah, I'm not really dead."

"In the name of God. Is that you? Nathan? I heard you died."

"Somewhat exaggerated," Stone said.

"Fuck. You're not dead?"

"Not yet. Look, this is way out of left field, and I know we haven't talked for years, but I need your help. Right now."

"I thought you had—"

"It's a long story. I'm nearby and I need help. Right now. Got an injured woman. Will you help me? I need to know one way or the other."

"Where are you?"

Stone told him.

"Marathon, eh . . . What happened?"

"Long story. She's been shot, soft tissue near the shoulder."

"Is she conscious?"

"No. She's also lost a lot of blood."

Barney groaned. "That's not good. What's wrong with the hospital?"

"I've got people on my tail. I need a favor. A really big favor. I'm calling them all in now. I need you."

A sigh. "Don't move. I'll be there in twenty minutes."

175

Barney was as good as his word. He reversed his pickup truck down onto the beach. Stone loaded Beatrice into the back. He climbed in beside her and held her hand.

"Keep your head down," Barney said, throwing a tarp over them.

The stoner kid dragged on his joint. "I hope she's okay, man. She looks blue."

Stone nodded. "Appreciate your help, son. I owe you one."

"Where's the ambulance?"

"We'll get her there first, don't worry."

Thirty minutes later they were at Barney's place near a beach on Lower Matecumbe Key.

The garage door opened automatically and they drove in. It shut behind them, and the lights flickered on.

"First stage complete," Barney said. "Let's get her inside."

Stone pulled back the tarp and carefully lifted Beatrice out of the back of the pickup. He followed Barney into an adjacent utility room. Then through another door into a large kitchen.

The blinds were all already drawn.

Barney flicked on the lights.

Stone laid Beatrice down gently on the wooden table.

"Boil some water, Nathan," Barney said. "A lot of hot water."

Stone did as he was told and poured the boiling water from the kettle into a bowl.

"You look like shit, Nathan," Barney said.

"Yeah, feel like shit."

"You smell like shit too."

"Been out in the fucking Everglades for days."

Barney washed his hands and switched on a stronger overhead light. He put on medical gloves. Then he put on a headlamp as he prepared to treat Beatrice's injuries.

He opened a black doctor's bag and took out some first-aid essentials, including disposable scalpels and iodine.

"This looks nasty," he said. "Helluva mess."

Stone watched as Barney cut the bloodstained bandage with scissors and then Beatrice's top, exposing her bare flesh. The light showed the splintered skin tissue around the shoulder. He injected a local anesthetic deep into her wound. He picked up a clean cloth, put some antibacterial soap on it, and dipped it in the boiling-hot water. He carefully swabbed the dirt and dried blood from the area. Then he sprayed an antibacterial spray into the wound to wash it out.

"Looks superficial," Stone said.

"Let's see." Barney washed it again with iodine. He peered at a quarter-inch-thick gash in the shoulder. "I can see a tiny little fragment. You see it?"

Stone looked closer at the wound and shrugged. "Can't see a thing."

"Just a tiny bit lodged near the tendon."

Stone thought he saw a sliver of gray bullet fragment. "Yeah, I think I see it."

"You know what I think?"

"What?"

"We leave it. We start slicing her open to pull it out, chances are it could cause more harm. She could easily bleed out. Go into shock. Die."

"So we're going to leave a bullet fragment inside her?"

"In the circumstances, that would be the smart thing."

"Won't that cause problems over time?"

"Perhaps in the longer term. But I can guarantee that without being in a trauma unit with access to arthroscopic equipment, she's better off with us simply cleaning it. I've got antibiotics and some excellent painkillers, and she can take a full course of them after I get her bandaged up."

Stone nodded. "Clean her up good."

Barney took twenty minutes to clean the wound until he was happy with it. Then he bandaged her up. He gave her smelling salts. A few moments later she came to, looking groggy, face ashen.

"What the fuck is happening? Who the fuck are you?" she asked, staring at Barney.

"Relax, honey," Barney said, "you lost a bit of blood. You need to rest up."

Beatrice looked up at Stone. "Why is my shirt off?"

Stone patiently explained what had happened and where they were.

Beatrice winced as she sat up on the table, Stone supporting her back. She looked at her bandaged shoulder. "You got something to cover me up?" she asked. "And something for this fucking pain."

Barney got a blanket and wrapped it around her. He gave her a couple of morphine tablets, a sleeping tablet, and a glass of cold water. She knocked them all back in one.

"How long have I been out of it?"

"Hour or more."

Beatrice looked around, eyes squinting as she winced in pain. "Are we back on the mainland? Please God."

"Yeah, not far from Marathon, Florida," Stone said, "down in the Keys. Take it easy."

"I made it?"

"Yeah, you made it. Now you need to sleep."

Within a few minutes, Beatrice was asleep on the table, wrapped up in the blanket.

Stone got the backpack and opened it up. He handed Barney the survivalist's $5,000 dollars in cash. "Take it."

"What the fuck is this?"

"For helping me out."

"I'm not taking your money."

"Take it!"

Barney reluctantly took it. "Are you kidding me? What's this for?"

"For helping us. But also I want to borrow your truck."

Barney shrugged. "Sure, take it. It's a piece of fucking junk anyway. But I don't want your money."

Stone smiled. "Shut up and take it. You're doing me a major favor."

"You look and smell like shit, man."

"Rough couple of days. And nights."

"With her? Who is she?"

Stone explained what had happened.

"Fuck, man . . . that's crazy. Flat-out crazy. She was hired to lure you into a trap?"

Stone nodded as he looked at the sleeping woman. "One hundred percent. She didn't know anything about it. She was set up too."

Barney poured himself and Stone double bourbons; there was a slight tremor in his hand. He knocked back the drink and closed his eyes. "Motherfucker, that's good."

Stone did the same. He felt the booze warm his insides.

"So, you're not dead. But your face is all different to how I remember."

"Long, long story."

"Which you don't want to share."

"It's not good."

"Well, just glad that you're still alive and kicking." Barney tapped the side of his glass. "You want another?"

"Maybe another time, Barney. I need to get her out of here."

"Already? Where the hell you going?"

"Someplace I can keep her safe and sound."

Barney looked at the woman wrapped in the blanket. "She's pretty."

Stone stared at her. She was twitching as if she was having a nightmare.

"Tell me about these guys. I still know some cops."

Stone shook his head. "Cops won't be able to save me or her if these guys find us."

Barney poured himself another double and knocked it back. "You want my advice? Get the hell out of Florida. At least for now."

"That's the plan. For now I'm going to lie low until she gets a bit stronger."

"I wish you all the best, Nathan. You need any help, I'll be there. I'm a shooter. I know all about guns, you know that."

"I know you do." Stone went quiet as his mind flashed through the searing events of the past few days. "Thanks, Barney."

Thirty-Eight

When Catherine Hudson's flight landed at Miami International Airport, she checked her cell phone. She had text messages from her husband. Her heart sank. He was wondering where she was. Was she coming home? What the hell was going on? Her daughter missed her. How long would she be gone for?

The more she thought about her home life, the more depressed she got. She knew her marriage was on the rocks. She was headed for divorce whether she liked it or not.

The fact of the matter was she couldn't truthfully answer any of her husband's or her daughter's questions. She claimed she had some "urgent business" to attend to in Florida. She imagined it made her appear like a psychotic workaholic, unable or unwilling to be more flexible and put her family first. Maybe John thought she was having an affair.

She wondered how long she could go on like this.

Catherine tried to push thoughts of her personal life to one side. She stepped outside into the sunshine, put on her sunglasses, and picked up her rental car. It felt good to feel the sun on her face. She began driving from the airport across Miami to an unassuming office block in Doral, used occasionally by CIA operatives. The specter of

Nathan Stone hung over her, making her more and more anxious with every passing minute.

The latest news was that Stone had made it out of the Everglades and was now down in the Keys. How was that even possible? Stone knew too much, but no one seemed capable of taking him out. Perhaps she had been wrong to insist on no collateral damage on the streets. Perhaps she should have stepped in and instructed Berenger to neutralize Stone in cold blood outside the bar. But hindsight was 20/20. Besides, she would have been going against the very core of the rationale that underpinned the Commission: they were autonomous. No direct links to the Agency.

She sensed that Stone hadn't finished humiliating them yet. Not by a long shot. It was as if he was enjoying himself, turning the table on his tormentors.

Her cell phone rang, and the Bluetooth in the car kicked in. She didn't recognize the caller ID.

"Catherine, hope you don't mind me cold-calling you." The voice belonged to Becky McFarlane.

Hudson felt a chill run down her spine. Her college friend had now been in touch twice in the space of a few days after nearly twenty years of silence. She wondered if she shouldn't just call her out, put an end to whatever subterfuge this was. But before she knew what she was doing, she was playing along, saying, "Becky, what a lovely surprise. Sorry, it was a bad line."

"I just wanted to see if you're free for lunch in the next week or so."

"Lunch?"

"I'm in DC real soon and was wondering if you wanted to meet up."

Hudson shook her head. "Absolutely," she lied. "That'd be great."

"So where are you now?" Becky asked.

Hudson thought that Becky was too nosy for her own good. "I'm down in Florida on business."

"I am so envious. You know how much I love the sun. Aargh . . . the weather in London is just the worst. Rain. Cloudy. And occasionally some sun. But only very occasionally."

"Sounds like Detroit on a good day."

"You're absolutely right. It's terrible. Anyway, just wanted to give you a heads-up. Is it okay if I call you in a couple days and we'll pick a time?"

Hudson seethed at the intrusion on her world. "That would be . . . perfect. Look, got to go, Becky. I'm on the highway. Catch up soon."

"Bye, Catherine!"

Hudson ended the call, surprised at how irritated she was at her old friend reentering her life at this moment. Even if Becky was being perfectly genuine, Hudson didn't in all honesty want to meet up with her again. Now she was facing some excruciating lunch or dinner listening to Becky talk about her perfect life while Hudson's disintegrated before her eyes.

Twenty minutes later she pulled up at an anonymous office building in Doral. She rode the elevator to the eighth floor and swiped her fake ID badge against a scanner.

Inside, the desk was already set up with a MacBook Pro. She made herself coffee and logged on to the CIA system. She gulped down the bitter brew, glad to get some more caffeine in her bloodstream.

Her cell phone rang. She didn't recognize the number.

"You in okay?" She didn't recognize the voice.

"Who is this?"

"My name's Figuel Cuetta, assigned to the State Department."

Hudson's guard was immediately up. Becky had previously worked for the State Department. Was this guy connected to her? "I'm listening."

"I'm a friend of Mr. Black's."

Hudson slumped back in her seat. "Go on."

"I'm two blocks from where you are. I work out of the State Department building here in Doral. But I'm Agency."

"I gathered that."

"I was asked to assist you."

"In what way?"

"I want to send someone over to you."

"Who?"

"He's a Brit."

"He's based in Miami?"

"Has been for fifteen years. Very discreet. Works only for us. Friend of Mr. Black's. Any work in and around Florida, he has it covered."

"He's a contractor?"

"That's exactly what he is. His company has half a dozen handpicked special forces operatives at his disposal. And they can be deployed as soon as he says so."

"Send him over."

The man was around six feet tall, late forties, clean shaven. He wore a black polo shirt, jeans, sneakers, and a chunky watch on his left wrist. He took a seat opposite her. His name was Reg Thomson, ex-SAS.

"You okay with me taking some notes?" he said.

"Sure."

Thomson took out a notebook and pen. "I believe you wanted to talk."

Hudson took a few minutes to give him the background on the situation. "It's not good."

Thomson flicked over a page of the notebook and began scribbling.

"What are your initial thoughts?"

"The first thought that comes to mind is why wasn't he just kidnapped outside the bar or shot in the head? What a fucking mess. He could've been wasted there and then."

"Yeah, no kidding. Unfortunately, the bar was within a stone's throw of the Miami Beach police station. We absolutely didn't want them involved. This guy, Nathan Stone, technically he doesn't exist."

Thomson nodded as if he were familiar with Stone's background.

"What concerns myself and Mr. Black now is the contagion. If this spreads, God knows where it could lead."

"You mean if Stone isn't neutralized?"

"Exactly. He knows too much. He's seen too much. He has background on this organization that we can't allow to get out. We need to shut him down for good."

The man nodded, taking a few more notes. "So just to be clear. You've got a fair-sized South African crew in place monitoring the situation."

"They have full operational control. We thought we had contained Stone and the girl out in the Everglades. But he's managed to get all the way to Marathon."

The man scribbled some more, shaking his head. "I've got to be straight-up honest with you, and no bullshit. This is ridiculous."

"I'm well aware of that, thank you."

"But it could also have, as you've said, terrible ramifications. The blowback from this would destroy the Agency."

"I want solutions, not a critique, thank you very much."

"Look, I don't mean to be on your case, or the guys who are trying to get Stone, but I mean, it's crazy that this has been allowed to go on so long."

Hudson shifted in her seat. "We don't want to be seen to intervene directly . . ."

"Well, you might have to. I think the time for being a spectator is over. Time to sort it out, even if it means neutralizing this guy on the street."

Hudson shook her head. "Not an option. In any shape or form."

"That comes from Mr. Black?"

"Yes, it does. And the people who green-lighted this program. But we need a contingency plan."

"A contingency plan if . . . ?"

"A contingency plan if the South African team can't take him down."

The man wrote some more and leaned back in his seat as he considered the situation Hudson was facing. "So, excuse me while I try and get up to speed. From what I've heard, this unit of South Africans, they've been using Sarasota, and they've got boots on the ground now, down in the Keys. Their operation takes precedence."

"One hundred percent correct. This is their thing."

"But if they fuck up again, we need to be ready. Is that what you're saying?"

Hudson nodded.

"So, what you're looking for is a parallel operation, lying in wait."

"Exactly."

Thomson was quiet for a few moments. "Are they an item these two, Stone and the girl?"

"We don't know. I don't think so. Why do you ask?"

"Well, if they're sleeping together, an anesthetic gas could be pumped into the air-conditioning system, knocking them both out. It would be easy to get them out, into a truck, and then take them away. Or it could be made to look like a drug overdose."

Hudson nodded. "That's exactly what we would be looking for. The first priority is to kill them both, but it needs to be done discreetly."

"And the second?"

Hudson frowned in confusion.

"You said the first priority is to kill Stone and the girl. What's the second priority?"

"Your involvement is on the proviso—and I think it's probably a long shot—that Stone escapes from the South African operatives. So . . . if you are called in, apart from neutralizing Stone, there are other people who will need to be disappeared. I'd like you to draw up plans when this meeting is over."

"People involved in the Commission?"

Hudson said only, "The buck has to stop somewhere."

"You got names?"

She nodded. "But not now. Not at this stage."

"Has this part two been green-lighted?"

"Not yet. But it will be."

Thomson nodded. "To be continued, then. Getting back to Stone, I have three guys available, highly capable guys who are here in Miami, people I know very well, and I can get them in place within a few hours. I'm talking top British operators. Very discreet."

"Good. You and you alone will speak to me. Your guys are not told about me or this place."

"That goes without saying. In terms of logistics, I'd like two guys down in the Keys, close by. They can monitor the situation from the sidelines, so to speak. But I'd like a presence."

"Okay, I like it."

"Also, I heard it was a drone that tracked him down."

Hudson tilted her head, curious. "How did you know that?"

"My company leased the drone to them. Caymans registered."

She let the information sink in. "Okay."

"What I would like is for the drone to be reactivated so that we can keep an eye on Stone via air, in addition to my two guys on the ground. But it costs."

"Just in case?"

The man nodded. "Means my guys don't have to run around and possibly alert Stone. Means they'll stay off the radar. Also means that by them not running around, they won't come to the attention of the South African guys."

"Electronic surveillance?"

"We'll be doing that as well. Of both Stone and the South Africans."

"You're not leaving anything to chance, are you?"

"Never do. That's why I'm still in business."

Thirty-Nine

Stone pulled up at a beach house on Cudjoe Key in the Lower Keys, a sedated Beatrice asleep in the passenger seat of Barney's pickup. He felt calmer than he had since the whole trip to Miami had gone to shit. This place was a safe house. He had bought the property for cash in the last year, along with a house in nearby Sugarloaf Key.

He had envisioned Helen one day moving into the Cudjoe house, with him living nearby. A place where she would be free. A place to call home. It was, for Nathan, a small way to pay back the enormous debt he felt he owed his sister. Her sacrifice. Her courage. She could paint. She could breathe the clean air. And feel the sun on her skin as a free woman for once. He knew deep down it was unlikely she would ever be released from the psychiatric hospital. But it felt good to know that she could have a place she could call her own if something ever happened to him.

Stone glanced at the sleeping Beatrice and smiled. He took the smelling salts Barney had given him out of his pocket, unscrewed the lid, and placed the bottle underneath Beatrice's nose.

She came to, eyes wide, before she winced in pain. "Fuck!" She looked out at the beach and sea. "How long have I been asleep?"

"A little while."

"Where am I? Where is this place?"

"Just a place I use from time to time. Do you want help into the house?"

Beatrice shook her head and grimaced as she got out of the truck, blanket still wrapped around her. He unlocked the front door, and she shuffled after him. It was all pastel colors and whites. She walked through and opened the french doors to the deck overlooking the ocean.

"Is this okay?" he asked.

"Are you kidding me, Jimmy? This is beautiful. Is this yours?"

"It's yours for as long as you want to be here."

"Why am I here?"

Stone smiled. "You'll be safe here. It's best if you stay here for a while."

Beatrice looked around. She unwrapped the blanket from her body.

Stone went to the closet and picked out a black linen shirt. He tossed it to her. "It's too big, but it'll do."

Beatrice looked at the fabric and put it on, grimacing with pain. "Thank you."

Stone handed her some morphine tablets. "This is for the pain. There's a Jeep outside. Keys are in the top drawer. Don't go too far. There's a phone."

"Where?"

Stone pointed to the kitchen. "It's on the wall. I've got the number. And only me. I'll contact you. But do not call out, clear?"

"Am I like a prisoner?"

"No. You're perfectly at liberty to go wherever you like."

Beatrice was quiet for a few moments. "I want to go back to my family in LA."

"You want to go back to LA, fine. You can take the Jeep and drive there."

"This is all too much to process . . . I feel a little woozy."

"That's natural."

"But I'm free to go? No bullshit?"

"You're free to go as of now. I swear. But I think it might be best for you to rest and recuperate before you head back to your family."

Beatrice looked around the whitewashed walls and winced, still heavily medicated. "I can't believe we made it." She shook her head. "I think I'm in the wrong business."

"It's comfortable. And quiet."

"I love it."

"There's a thousand bucks in a bottom drawer for emergencies. Groceries and stuff. But the fridge also has stuff in there, and there's bread, frozen food in the freezer, and all that."

"So—and I'm not trying to be smart—but I'm free to leave at any time?"

Stone pointed to the sofa. "Sit down and relax."

Beatrice sat down as Stone got her a glass of sparkling water. "Thank you."

Stone sat on the edge of the sofa. "First, you've done amazing getting through all this shit. Second, you are absolutely free to go. I keep my word. I just wanted to bring you here so that you could recuperate at your own pace."

"Very nice of you." She gave a tired smile. "The guys who are after you . . ."

"Yeah, what about them?"

"I want you to be straight with me. Don't lie."

Stone nodded.

"These guys . . . would they find me in LA?"

"What do you want to hear?"

"I don't understand."

"Do you want to hear what you want to hear? Yeah, everything's going to be fine. Fingers crossed. Or do you want the truth? Unvarnished."

"I want the goddamn truth, unvarnished."

Stone sighed. "I've said it before, and I'll say it again. You can head back to LA. Go to the cops. And I don't doubt you would live. But for how long, I don't know."

Beatrice closed her eyes.

"If you're lucky, they'll find you and kill you quick."

"Are you serious?"

Stone nodded. "These are dangerous people. They kill people. They're a lot like me."

"I miss my daughter. I can't bear being away from her."

Stone nodded.

"I want to see her. But I don't want to put her at risk. I need to know . . . Would they kill my daughter?"

"I don't know. Possibly."

Beatrice ran her hands through her tangled hair. "What a nightmare."

"Listen to me. Until you figure out your next move, you'll be safe here."

"Promise?"

"Yes, I promise. They don't know about this place. I think we lost them after their boat blew up."

"Good."

"Beatrice, I'm very careful. This property isn't even in my name. It's under the name of a company."

"That's good. And there's a phone?"

"Kitchen. But if you call the cops when I leave, these guys who were on our tail will find you for sure. They will be tracing all calls to the local police, and they've probably wiretapped the phones of everyone you know."

Beatrice nodded.

"If you want to go to the cops, fine, that's your choice. But I would strongly advise you against it. At least at this stage. Your name will pop up in numerous systems across the country, some more secure than others."

"What about calls to my daughter?"

"Aren't you paying attention? Absolutely not. Not now. Maybe once this is over."

"And when will it be over?"

Stone shrugged. "I don't know. I do know that chilling out here, recuperating, relaxing will do you a world of good."

"So you're not going to stay here with me?"

Stone shook his head. "Treat this as your home for as long as you're here."

"And this is yours?"

Stone nodded. "I move around. Like to spend time here in the winter if I can. My sister's at a hospital up in Homestead, so I'm close enough too."

"I need a shower."

"Shower here. But I would wait till tomorrow. Then take off the bandage. First-aid kit underneath the sink in the kitchen. Antiseptic spray, and you've got morphine and antibiotic pills."

Beatrice smiled. "I can't believe what the hell I've been through. What we've been through."

Stone got to his feet. "One final thing." He went to the bedroom and opened a safe inside the closet. He pulled out a cell phone and handed it to her. "Do not use this."

"So, what's the point of giving it to me?"

"I've got a plan. But you need to keep this phone on you. Set it to vibrate, keep it in your pocket. When it vibrates, it means I've sent you a message. You follow what it says to the letter if I message you. Do not ignore it. If I contact you, you need to see what I'm saying."

Beatrice looked unsure. Her gaze wandered around the room. On a duck-egg-blue wooden bookshelf in the corner was an old black-and-white photo. She walked over to the photo and lifted it. It showed a young boy and a stick-thin woman with a swollen eye. "Is this you?" she said.

Stone nodded.

"And this is . . . your mother?"

"Yeah. I was about four at the time. She left a few weeks after that was taken."

"I'm sorry."

Stone sighed. "My father was an alcoholic. He beat her senseless. Leaving was the only way she could see to survive."

Beatrice touched the glass and looked up. "That's how my husband left me on many a night, let me tell you. Good-for-nothing bastard."

"He beat you?"

"He beat me bad."

"I'm sorry."

"He used to have a coke addiction. Got clean. But he's still a bastard in my eyes."

"And he's got custody?"

"I see her once a month. Supervised visit. It's something." Beatrice looked again at the picture. "You look so sad."

"So does my mother."

"Where was this taken?"

"Down the street from Katz's Deli. You know, the one you hadn't heard of."

Beatrice rolled her eyes. "I'll never forget it now, believe me."

"It's all in the past now. We need to focus on the present."

Beatrice smiled. "And I'll be okay here?"

"Yes. Rest up. And I'll be back to see you."

Forty

De Boer was sitting in the back of an SUV as his new second-in-command, Joseph Salerno, trained a telephoto lens on Nathan Stone, almost half a mile away, as the target drove off from the house in Cudjoe Key. The drone had monitored Stone and the girl from off the coast of Marathon until they were taken away by a guy in a pickup truck.

His team had learned that the vehicle was registered to a former cop, Barney McKeever. A loser who had been fired for being drunk on duty fifteen years earlier. A veteran who had lived alone since his wife left him. They knew where McKeever lived, and now, having followed the truck when it left Marathon, they knew where the girl was.

De Boer's men could have followed Stone, but the death of Pieter had made him more cautious. The last thing he needed was a confrontation with Stone getting out of hand on the mainland. They needed to play it safe. They knew that the girl was in Cudjoe and that he would return to see her. When the time was right, they would finally get him and the girl together, without turning it into a war zone.

"He's a nasty bastard," Salerno said. "Why didn't he kill her?"

"Good question," de Boer answered. "I've been wondering that myself."

"Doesn't seem like the Nathan Stone I've heard about." Salerno rubbed his face as if frustrated at the lack of action. "I say we should have followed him. We could have stabbed the fucker there and then. Sniper shot. All kinds of options."

"We can't have him bleeding out in public in the middle of the day."

Salerno shook his head. "I say we should have shanked the fuck."

"You underestimate him. Look where that got us with Pieter and then Bakker out in the fucking Everglades."

"Point taken. Sorry, you're right."

"I want him dead more than anyone, trust me. But we do this correctly and we achieve all our objectives. And get the fuck out of here and back home." De Boer was quiet for a few moments.

Salerno asked, "What are you thinking about?"

"I'm thinking about Pieter. His wife doesn't know yet. Neither do my parents."

"Shit. When you going to deal with that side of things?"

"When Stone is gone. When this mess is finally finished. Then, and only then, can I think about that."

De Boer's cell phone rang.

"Kevin." The voice belonged to Berenger. "Where are we?"

"Stone just left a nice little beach house in Cudjoe. He dropped off the girl."

There was silence on the line, as if Berenger was weighing the significance of Stone's actions. "Why would he do that?"

"I know, it's weird."

"I don't get it. Do we have any rationale for why he's keeping her there?"

"She might be terrified and doing exactly what he says. That's why she's staying put. He left a few minutes ago."

Berenger swore. "Why hasn't he been taken out?"

De Boer sighed. "We don't want another fuck-up, okay? The kind of fuck-up that got my brother killed. We do things slow. Methodical. We don't want a bloodbath. I've had my fill of this fuck."

"Kevin, I understand your caution. But the job has to be completed now that we know where they are."

"I'm in operational charge. And I say how we work this. He doesn't know that we've tracked them down. He couldn't have been aware of the drone. And he sure as hell wouldn't have left the girl alone if he'd known."

"Unless he's hoping we kill her."

"No, not buying that."

Berenger sighed. "So, what's the plan?"

"We need to do it clean. Easiest thing in the world would be to kill them inside the house. It'll look like a double murder. The problem is that doesn't happen in the Keys, at least not often. That's when you get blowback. Serious fucking blowback. All sorts of attention you don't need."

"Agreed. What we need is for them to disappear. That's the best kind of hit. They just disappear. As if they were never there."

"You will have him, Mark. Believe me, I'd love to just grab the fucker and shoot him, pay him back for killing Pieter. But it's about picking the right moment. We're working on an operational plan as we speak. When it's done, we go."

"All right," Berenger said. "Let me know when this is finished."

De Boer ended the call and turned to Salerno. "How you feeling?"

"I want to get some action. All the boys do."

De Boer stared at the cottage. "Think I have a little job for you and your friends to keep you occupied in the meantime."

Forty-One

Stone felt uneasy leaving Beatrice at the cottage on Cudjoe. There was a risk that she was going to freak out and go straight to the police. But he needed some time away. He had to figure out his next move.

He headed straight to Lower Sugarloaf Key, a short drive away. He pulled up outside his other house, a four-bedroom, conch-style house on Bonefish Lane West.

Stone had registered the house under the name Helen O'Farrell, his mother's maiden name. He bent down and picked up the key from under a rock next to the bushes in front of the window.

He opened the door, went inside, and locked the door behind him. He took a few moments to enjoy the silence—the constant talking was one thing he wouldn't miss about Beatrice.

After he showered and dressed, Stone pulled down the blinds and lay back on the sofa. He needed to sleep to recharge his batteries. He closed his eyes.

His mind flashed back to the bar in South Beach where it had all begun. The Everglades. Beatrice getting attacked, then shot. And still trusting him.

His mind flashed to the photo she'd seen of him and his mother on the Lower East Side all those years ago. His mother had disappeared without any notice. Without a word. Without a kiss. Was that how

Beatrice's daughter would remember things if she didn't make it back home?

The rage Stone had felt at being abandoned, left at the mercy of his psychotic father, still burned deep within him. But he had learned to deal with it better. Slowly, over the years, he had rationalized his mother's abandonment. More or less. It was true what he'd told Beatrice. He didn't blame his mother. Her choice was purely one of survival. If she had stayed, she would be dead.

He sometimes wondered what had happened to her. Was she still alive? He imagined her in the Pacific Northwest, remarried, maybe even with pictures of Nathan and his sister tucked away in a drawer somewhere. Maybe they were gathering dust in an attic. A reminder that her children existed. But they weren't just ghosts from her past. They were flesh and blood.

Stone felt himself drifting off. Deeper and deeper into a dreamless sleep.

The sun was shining in through the closed blinds when he woke. Stone stirred and got his bearings. He got up, went to the bathroom, splashed cold water on his face, brushed his teeth, and popped three steroid-and-amphetamine pills. He washed them down with a glass of cold water, then stared at his reflection in the mirror. The new face, specially crafted by plastic surgeons in Saudi Arabia, still looked strange to him, even after all this time. He still hadn't accepted it. It looked like someone else.

He began to think about what lay ahead for him that day. He felt the adrenaline begin to surge. The edge was returning. He was mentally attuned to what he needed to do. A plan was in place. A new plan. He needed to get Beatrice to safety. But he also needed to consider the people who had been following them from Miami out to the Everglades. Whether they'd been able to track him after he blew up their boat was something he needed to know before he could move forward.

Stone got in Barney's pickup truck and drove across to nearby Sugarloaf Lodge. He wolfed down a huge burger, fries, and a large Coke. Then he ordered a margherita pizza and four cans of Diet Coke. The waitress looked at him as if there was something wrong with him.

An idea was beginning to form as his mind got sharper. He ran the scenarios through his head before he acted.

Stone called the number of his house in Cudjoe.

The phone rang seven times before Beatrice picked up. "Hello?" Her voice was tentative.

"Hi. Wanted to give you a call to see if you're okay."

"I was terrified to pick up."

"How's the shoulder?"

"Hurts like a bitch," she said.

"It'll take a few days to settle down. Have you taken the morphine pill?"

"Yeah, just took one a few minutes ago."

"Good. You'll be feeling better in an hour or so."

"I hope so. This pain's driving me nuts."

"Other than that, how are you?"

"Just been sleeping. I feel kinda shitty, actually, if you must know."

"Scared?"

"A little. Actually, a lot."

Stone laughed. "That's natural. It happens. It'll pass."

"What the fuck is so funny?" she said.

"You. You worry too much."

"Of course I worry. What the hell is wrong with you? This *is* worrying. Do you understand?"

"Sure."

"I don't know if you do. I'm going to have to change my name, my life, start again."

"Was your old life so great?"

"No . . . it wasn't, if I'm being honest. But it was a life. My life. Now? Now . . . I'm scared. I want to get out of here. I feel like a sitting duck."

"We'll get you out. Have you eaten anything?"

"Yeah, I had some food. And drank gallons of water."

"That's good."

"I don't have any clothes."

"If you want, go down to Key West, pick up some clothes, and then head back to the house. You're only twenty minutes away."

"Now?"

"Why not?"

"Is that okay?"

"Do not use credit cards. Use the cash I gave you."

"Are you sure?"

"Yes. And we can meet up later. I'll give you a call."

"Is this a date?"

"I wouldn't call it that."

"So what is it, then? A drink? A meal?"

"We could do both."

A beat passed. "How long until it's safe for me to go back to my family?"

"I don't want to lie to you. It might be a while. But how about we meet up tonight and talk? Face-to-face. Me and you. Whatever's on your mind. I'll tell you how I think you can move forward, and you can tell me your thoughts."

"And I can go to Key West?"

"What's stopping you? You've got the Jeep, some cash, and it's only a twenty-minute drive. It's easy."

"What about you?"

"What about me?"

"What are you going to do?"

"Pick up some provisions," he lied. "Will you be okay to drive with your shoulder?"

"I'm fine . . . In the meantime, though, I'm going to have to use some old chinos of yours, tie them tight with a belt, and roll up the bottom."

"Borrow whatever you want. Gotta go."

"And you'll call me tonight?"

"I promise."

Forty-Two

Catherine Hudson was staring out of the windows of her office in Doral, contemplating the ongoing operation down in the Keys. She sensed they were reaching the endgame. Finally. She wanted the whole thing to be over.

The more she thought about how messed up things had gotten, both in the operation and her private life, the more she wondered if she shouldn't be considering resigning. Suddenly, being a stay-at-home mom seemed more attractive than negotiating the quagmire that had become the Commission.

Hudson was surprised the thought had even crossed her mind. She had begun to consider her future without the Agency. She felt sick at how out of control things had gotten. The deaths of the members of the Commission in New York last year had shocked her to her core.

Deep down, she began to wonder if Stone would find her too. Was that too much of a stretch?

Hudson felt a pain in her temple. Another migraine. She popped a couple of Advil and washed them down with some cold coffee.

Her cell phone rang, and Hudson checked the caller ID. She saw her boss's name, and her stomach tightened.

"Catherine," Black said. "Sorry, I was in a meeting when you called earlier."

"Sir, it was an update on the Everglades."

Black sighed. "Jeez . . . isn't this over yet?"

"Not quite, but soon, I believe."

Hudson relayed the information from the intercepted call that Stone was going to be meeting up with the actress that evening in the Keys. She also let him know that the woman was headed down to Key West to do some shopping.

"That sounds like the best break we've had in days. We need to get this done."

"I don't know."

"What's the problem?"

Hudson looked at the dashcam feed from de Boer's SUV in the Lower Keys. "I don't like it. Maybe Stone has me spooked, I don't know. It almost feels too easy."

"Let's try and not overthink this. We get to the location and we end this."

Hudson sighed. "I hope you're right. Maybe I'm just frazzled. It's all been a lot to handle, to be honest."

"Are you okay, Catherine? You don't sound quite like your usual self. You don't sound like you're in a good place."

"Honestly, sir, I'm not. This thing has thrown me for a loop. But I want to reassure you that I'm on it. I'll get this mess cleaned up. One way or the other."

"Is there anything else?"

Hudson closed her eyes and sighed. "It's also . . ." She watched the images from the SUV. It was on the move again. "Just an old college friend. Remember I mentioned her . . ."

"Yeah, the one in London?"

"Right. Well, she gave me a call saying she wanted to meet up again in DC. It all sounds strange."

Black was silent for a few moments, as if contemplating his answer. "Tell me what's really bothering you about this, Catherine."

Hudson sighed. "Sir, I think part of me is wondering if this relates to my work."

"What makes you think that?"

"I'm wondering if she's Agency too. I guess that's what's bothering me."

Black didn't answer.

"I'm wondering if her State Department role is cover."

Black sighed. "I don't know anything about her. And I know a lot of people and everything that's going on."

"I'm sorry to bother you with this. It feels strange to even be raising this question."

"It's fine. We've all been there. Had our doubts. Bad days. Bad weeks. We envision things that aren't quite as they seem. I get it. But somehow we manage to muddle through in the end."

Hudson felt tears on her cheeks. She was angry with herself for allowing her emotions to come to the surface.

"We need to press on. Do what has to be done. And live to fight another day."

"You're absolutely right, sir. And I appreciate your time on this."

Black paused, then added, "I think you need a vacation when this is over, Catherine. Overthinking things is always a sign you need a break. Take some time off. What do you say?"

"I have too much going on, sir."

"When was the last time you took a vacation?"

"Couple of years ago."

"Three years. I checked. You need to unwind and get your mojo back."

"Yeah, maybe you're right."

"On a related note, at the meeting I was just in I was discussing the Commission with a couple of my senior colleagues—men I trust, men with great judgment—who are aware of what is going on. We talked it over at length. The meeting lasted almost four hours. And I relayed to them your concerns and that it might be time to wind up the operation."

Hudson sat down in her chair and leaned back, gazing at the feed from de Boer's team as they followed the actress. She was in a Jeep, driving down US 1 toward Key West. "I'm listening, sir."

"They, like me, believe that the Commission is a great vehicle to allow us to shape the political and economic landscape. And so it would be premature to abandon that project. Premature in the extreme."

Hudson feared that would be the response. "If that's the case, then I suggest the two constants, our friend in Wyoming and Dr. Berenger, be replaced. That's how I see things moving forward."

There was a lengthy silence. Hudson sensed that she had either said something wrong or something terribly presumptuous.

"What I mean by that, sir, is that new people who aren't linked to the previous iterations of the Commission could be recruited and a new wealthy backer put in place. I'm sure it wouldn't be hard finding new blood whose aims align with ours."

A beat. "You know, Catherine, this world we inhabit, sometimes there's no right or wrong. No black or white. It's usually gray. What I mean by that—and bear with me while I go off on a tangent—is that our business is rarely so cut and dried. It's always a winding route to the final destination, so to speak. You know who told me that?"

Hudson wondered where her boss was going with his musings. "I don't know, sir."

"It was your grandfather."

"It sounds like the sort of thing he would say."

"He was a master of sensing what needed to be done while also realizing there were different and surprising paths to the destination."

"Indeed."

"Catherine, your grandfather taught me everything I know about the business we're in. The obligations. The sacrifices. And you know what else he said?"

"What's that, sir?"

"We must always subsume our egos, our personalities, wishes, and desires for the mission. For the country. For the flag. What he meant is that we shouldn't get sentimental about the harsh decisions that have to be made. Eisenhower said it best. Sometimes it is a *distasteful but vital necessity.* We all make these decisions. Our heart might be breaking at the course of action we're forced to take. But we push those thoughts aside because we must allow this country to flourish, to be free, and we have to see the big picture."

"Absolutely, sir."

"We all know that the National Security Act of 1947 gave us five main functions."

"That's right, sir."

"Four pertain to the collection and dissemination of intelligence."

Hudson sensed he was going to be talking about the other function. The fifth.

"What you and I are involved with," Black said, "are very sensitive aspects of our work. Work your grandfather excelled at. I remember he referred to a quote in the act, that the CIA is to *perform such other functions and duties related to intelligence affecting the national security as the National Security Council may from time to time direct.*"

"He used to quote the same passage to me, sir."

Black laughed. "I bet he did. My point is, the CIA is allowed to conduct operations that are secret, insomuch as our country's national security is at risk or is perceived to be at risk. And entities like the Commission fall under that umbrella. Your idea was brilliant. Americans can't know everything that's going on. How could they? They're too busy enjoying their liberty and freedom. But getting back to the Commission, we are clear that it shall remain intact—"

"Even in its current form?"

A pause. "We will consider all options. But only after this mission is complete."

"Thank you, sir."

"Tell me, Catherine—and I won't keep you too long, since I know you have pressing matters to deal with down in Florida—you know the gentleman in Wyoming quite well, don't you?"

Hudson shifted in her seat, surprised at the question. "Fisk? He's an old family friend, sir. I think I explained that at the outset."

"You did indeed. And that made your proposal all the more persuasive. Fisk is a patriot. A true American." Black sighed. "I remember your grandfather mentioned that Fisk's own father, a Texas oilman, had made some gasoline invention way back in the day and became one of the country's first billionaires. And a founder of the John Birch Society, apparently."

Hudson went quiet. She wondered if Fisk's power and influence, especially within the highest echelons of the CIA, were far more entrenched than she had imagined. She sensed from Black's tone that any move to oust Fisk would not be countenanced. But why? Was Fisk untouchable? Slowly it began to dawn on her. How could she have been so stupid? Fisk wasn't only a valuable CIA asset; he had probably been working for the Agency all along. Perhaps for decades. How could she have misread Fisk's role? She had assumed he could be removed if and when she said so. But it was clear Fisk was not in any danger of losing his role. Far from it. She was the one who was actually at risk.

"Fisk's father was a smart man," Black said.

"Indeed he was, sir."

"He saw earlier than just about anyone in America the threat from the Soviet Union, now Russia. But he also saw the threat from communism. He despised it. A visceral hatred of the state and state intervention. The same traits are there in his son, John Fisk Jr."

Hudson said nothing.

"How well do you know Fisk?"

"Well . . . when I was younger I occasionally went with my grandfather on his visits to meet him down in Florida. Once in Wyoming."

"What was your abiding memory?"

"I was allowed to get some chocolate ice cream. That's all I was interested in."

"Catherine, I'm glad you have a backup plan in place. My British friend Thomson is someone worth knowing."

The abrupt change in topic threw her off balance once again, leaving her certain she'd said the wrong thing. "Yes, sir."

"And when Stone and the woman are out of the picture, give me a call. We'll draw up new plans for the Commission going forward."

Hudson began to realize she was no longer calling the shots. It felt like a betrayal. An overwhelming sense of foreboding washed over her. "What kind of plans, sir?"

"You'll see."

The line went dead.

Forty-Three

Stone filled Barney's pickup with gas, bought a pair of sunglasses, and headed north on US 1. He planned to return the vehicle to Barney, an hour's drive away. Then he hoped Barney would be able to drop him back in the Lower Keys. If not, he could rent a car in nearby Islamorada before meeting up with Beatrice that night.

The truck's window was down. The salty breeze felt good on his skin. He always loved driving on the Overseas Highway, the beautiful blue Gulf waters below. It felt like being suspended in time. He drove past Marathon and then farther up the Keys, past sleeping towns, villages, and roadside food shacks.

When he pulled up outside Barney's home, he looked around. Nice, peaceful area. He locked the pickup and knocked on the front door.

Stone waited a few moments, since he knew Barney had suffered partial deafness in one ear after a shell exploded close to him in Vietnam. He knocked again. But still there was no answer.

Stone opened the mail slot and shouted, "Hey, Barney, you decent? I'm returning your pickup."

He knocked a few more times. Still no answer.

He knew Barney liked to relax on his deck, maybe drinking a beer or two. Watching a ball game. He wondered whether he should just push the keys through the mail slot. Then again, he wanted to thank his friend.

Stone looked at the key ring and saw what looked like a front door key attached to it. He tried it in the lock, turned the handle, and the door opened. He assumed Barney had a spare set.

Stone looked around the hallway. "Barney, it's Nathan. Sorry to barge in. Got your truck. Just dropping off your keys."

Nathan headed into the living room. Looked around. It was all neat pastel colors. The smell of fresh furniture polish. He hadn't figured Barney as the house-proud type.

"Barney, it's Nathan. I've got your keys. I let myself in. You decent, you old bastard?"

Stone searched all over the house. No sign of Barney. He wondered if Barney had left in another vehicle. Had Barney gone for a drink at a local bar?

Stone headed out into the back garden and looked around. Neat lawn, high wooden fence. Wooden shed. No Barney.

He went back into the house. Headed into the utility room, where there was a washing machine and dryer and the door that led to the garage.

Stone turned the handle, but it was locked. He banged on the door. "Barney, it's Nathan. You in there? You fall asleep?"

No answer.

Stone looked at the key ring. It held only the pickup keys and the front door key. He turned the handle again and pushed hard. But the door didn't budge. He wondered if Barney had had a heart attack tinkering with one of the old engines he liked to repair. He shoved the door hard with his shoulder. It opened slightly. "Goddamn!"

He pushed harder and harder until the door to the garage began to give. He wondered what was jamming it. Was it Barney? Had he collapsed?

Stone's gaze was drawn to a speck of red on the tiled floor. Had to be blood.

He pushed the door wider with all his strength. Inside the garage, curled in a ball against the door, was the bloodied and battered body of Barney.

Forty-Four

When Stone finally managed to get into the garage, he could see Barney had been wedged completely against the door. He stepped over Barney's body and kneeled down beside his friend's lifeless form. His mouth was twisted, as if he were in pain. His eyes were bloodshot and wide, staring at something in horror. Stone could see stab wounds to the throat and neck. Barney's fingers crushed and bloodied. Stone turned and saw a workbench vise. Had his hands been placed in that? His head?

Stone felt his initial physiological reaction moving from shock to raw anger. A dark, terrible anger was brewing deep within him. Jolts of adrenaline rushing into his body.

The Commission had murdered Barney. It had to be them. They had managed to track Stone and Beatrice to the Keys after all. How was that possible? Barney was always careful to make sure he wasn't being followed. Had they been followed from the moment Barney picked them up on Sombrero Beach in Marathon?

Stone replayed the scene again and again in his head and wondered how that could have been possible. There was no one there. Just that stoner kid.

The more he thought about it, the more he realized they had somehow seen Stone come ashore in the Keys. How, he didn't know. But they had. Somehow.

It would have been relatively straightforward to follow Barney to his house. But he couldn't remember any car following them. None at all. Was there some surveillance footage in or around Sombrero Beach that had been triggered with facial recognition software? Was that it? Fuck.

But then why kill Barney? As a warning for Stone? Or were they just getting their kicks? Maybe they hadn't expected Stone to turn up at Barney's door so soon. Barney had obviously been tortured. Because they wanted to find out what he knew? How Barney knew Stone?

He stared down at the grizzled, battered, bloodied, twisted mess that had been his friend. Stone didn't do friends as a rule, but he wouldn't hesitate to call Barney one.

"I'll find the fuckers who did this, Barney," he said. Stone peered into his friend's blank, dead eyes, feeling terrible that Barney had suffered for helping him out. "You have my word."

Stone headed back into the house and looked around. He went upstairs and into a bedroom. There was a picture of Barney as a young man in Vietnam, smoking a cigarette. On the back of the photo it simply said, *Mekong Delta, 1967*. Other pictures beside his bed showed him with his wife and daughter, both of whom had been estranged from him for years, according to Barney.

Stone stared out of the back bedroom window to the neat garden and the sun-bleached lawn. A feeling of dread washed over him. He wondered if they had tracked down Beatrice too. But Barney didn't know about the beach house in Cudjoe. That was something.

His gaze was drawn to the shed at the bottom of the garden. He remembered Barney had said it was his work base where he repaired old bikes. He made a few bucks doing that. Barney was a Harley-Davidson fanatic. He loved everything about the bikes. The machinery. The care and attention to detail. But more than anything, he loved the fact that the bikes were 100 percent American made. Barney was a true patriot. That he died in such circumstances was killing Stone inside. He was responsible.

He headed outside to the back garden to get some fresh air. He walked up to the shed and tried the handle. It was locked. He wanted to see inside more out of curiosity than anything. He headed back inside to the utility room. A rusty key with a piece of string attached to it hung from a nail on a plasterboard wall.

Stone took the key, which opened the creaking door of the shed. Inside, he saw a workbench. Lying around it were welding goggles, a digital radio, and some oily rags. In the corner was the tarp that had covered Stone and Beatrice the previous night in the pickup.

Nathan pulled back the tarpaulin, revealing a 1980s Harley-Davidson with state trooper paint and markings. Hanging on a nail was a garment bag. He unzipped it. Inside was an old-style motorcycle cop uniform.

Stone wondered how Barney had managed to keep hold of this gear after he was let go from the force for excessive drinking. Had the cops allowed him to keep the motorcycle as a memento? Then again, maybe he'd bought it all on eBay. Thinking back to better days.

Stone flashed back to the first time he'd met Barney. It was a decade earlier. A bar in Key West. Barney had got to talking. Stone didn't want to talk. Eventually, Barney had bought him a drink. Stone felt compelled to buy him one back. Within a couple of hours, they were sharing stories about the army. Stone listened as Barney talked about Vietnam. The terror of night patrols. Being eaten alive by ants. Trapped in jungle firefights. Scared out of his wits. They had kept in touch after that until Stone had nearly drowned a few years back during that fucked-up operation in the Everglades that had ended with him getting plastic surgery in Saudi Arabia.

Stone's mind snapped back to the present. He had been formulating a plan for getting Beatrice to safety. But Barney's murder meant he would have to adjust his plans.

It was then, in that moment of reflection, that a germ of an idea began to form. It was rough. It was dangerous. It was a high-risk strategy. But the more he thought about it, the more excited he got.

Stone stood in the shed and looked around the confined space. He began to contemplate a move. A move that would get revenge for Barney. The high-risk strategy forming in his head at that moment was a way for him to escape from the Commission's clutches. But it was also a way to get the bastards out of Beatrice's life forever.

Suddenly, he could see the plan with staggering clarity. He mentally worked through the steps, closing his eyes as he envisioned each possible path and his response.

Stone pulled up a seat in the shed and sat in silence for nearly an hour, thinking and planning. Satisfied that he now knew what to do, he took out his cell phone and called his Cudjoe home.

"Hello?" Beatrice answered.

"Only me," Stone said. "You back already?"

"Picked up what I needed and headed straight back. After what you said, I thought that would be the smart thing to do."

Stone sighed. "Listen, do you still want to have a drink and bite to eat?"

"Yeah. Can we also talk about when I can finally go home? That's top of my list. I need to see my daughter. My family."

Stone cleared his throat. "Not a problem. We'll talk about that. Absolutely."

"I can't believe I'm having this conversation."

"What do you mean?"

"I don't know. This is all very surreal."

Stone said nothing.

"So, where do you have in mind?" she asked.

Stone cleared his throat. "There's a really nice place. It's called the No Name Pub. Big Pine Key."

"Is this some sort of joke?"

"Seriously, that's what it's called. Cool place. It's only about ten miles away from you."

"What time?"

"Let's make it nine p.m. So you should leave at eight forty-five."

"That's very precise."

"I'm a precise person. That's why we're both still alive. Don't leave until eight forty-five."

"Is there any reason why I shouldn't leave until then?"

A beat. "'Cause I say so. Plus, I don't want you hanging around."

"Got it."

"What will you be wearing?" Stone asked.

"I'm sorry, what?"

"You got a T-shirt?"

"I've got a new floral-patterned dress."

"What color are the shoes you'll be wearing?"

"What's that got to do with anything?"

"Simple question."

"Are you messing with me?"

"No, I'm not messing with you. I'm asking you what shoes you'll be wearing."

"Have you got a fetish about shoes? Is that it?"

"Not at all. Can you answer my question?"

"Red flats. Happy?"

"Good," Stone said. "Tell me again what the plan is?"

"Why?" she said. "You told me."

"Just so I know you're clear."

"I'm headed to the No Name Pub on Big Pine Key, nine o'clock tonight. But I don't leave until eight forty-five. Is that right?"

"Perfect."

Beatrice sighed. "I so want to go home."

"I know you do. And you will. Just be a little more patient. I'm working things out. Do you trust me?"

"I guess I'll have to."

"See you tonight."

Forty-Five

De Boer sat in the back of a white van with three members of his team in a parking lot in Cudjoe, giving them an ideal line of sight to the beach house where the actress was staying. He checked the monitors for any sign of movement. But still nothing.

Two other teams were close by, awaiting instructions.

De Boer turned to Craig Thornton, who was looking pensive. "What are you thinking?"

Thornton had been South African special forces for nearly a decade. He was deep in thought. "I don't know."

"What's the problem? I think this is shaping up nicely, don't you?"

Thornton sighed. "Perhaps too nicely."

"I don't follow."

"Nathan Stone is one of these guys who just seems to sense danger. He's alert to it."

"We tracked him down. We've got him in the kill box."

"We don't know where he is just now. Not definitively."

"We know where he's headed tonight. And the time and place. I'm happy with that."

Thornton sat quietly, lost in his thoughts. "True."

"He won't be expecting us. The fact that he called the girl shows he's let his guard down."

Thornton sighed. "I hope you're right, man."

De Boer realized he was grinding his teeth. He wanted to wipe out both Stone and the girl and get back on a plane to South Africa. Finally wallow in the grief of losing Pieter.

Thornton stared out of a small window in the back of the van. "Kevin, how long have you known me?"

"A long time."

"A long, long time. We know this stuff. And we've all met guys like Stone. We're not too dissimilar from him. But he's something else. I think we should've just killed the girl. And then gotten Stone. Separately. We could still do that. She's in there."

De Boer shook his head. "The element of surprise is what we have going in our favor. We know what time they're meeting up tonight. He won't know that we've traced her to this house. The strategy is perfect."

"That's where I think you're wrong. By waiting till we think we have the right moment, we're giving him more space to maneuver around us."

"We're creating the illusion that all is well. Tonight we get them both. At the same place. We will destroy this bastard once and for all. I hate the fucker. I want to rip his fucking head off."

Thornton rubbed his face with his hands. "I don't like it. I just don't like it. Something feels wrong."

"What *exactly* feels wrong?" de Boer snapped.

"Hey, chill, man. I just think you're being too cautious."

"Craig, you've been in this business as long as I have. One thing I've learned is tactical patience."

"Don't be giving me a goddamn lecture, man."

"Fine. So let's focus on the plan. We got the guys in place?"

"Yeah, one in the pub, two at the tables outside, and two more in an SUV nearby."

"And you did Stone's buddy Barney good?"

"Sure did."

"You're going to be doing it all again tonight. You've got a taste for it, don't you? Felt good?"

Thornton nodded. "Felt good."

"Let's talk tonight's scenario through again. I want us all to be on the same page."

"Sure."

De Boer pictured the scene. "If they're both in the bar enjoying a cold one, tell me again, how do we neutralize them? What would you do, Craig? Just want your thoughts on what you'd do. Not what *I* think we should do."

"Masks, wait till they come outside, silencer, shots to the head when they leave. Drop a bag of coke at the scene. Drug deal gone wrong. Then we're off."

De Boer nodded. "No point in taking them down inside the bar?"

Thornton shook his head. "It's open till midnight. So we're hoping it'll just be them settling in for some booze."

"Then again, might be one drink, then off. Going to get ugly if there are other customers outside."

"Collateral damage. I'm ready for anything. You know that."

De Boer was deep in thought. "What about this . . . ? When Stone arrives, two of our guys wearing masks are waiting in the parking lot. They shoot him point-blank with a 9mm with a silencer when he gets out of his vehicle. Then they disappear. But then the guy in the bar takes out the girl and the bar staff and any customers."

"That's nice. I like that a lot. Sadly, collateral damage. But it means Stone is taken out quickly. We're not fucking around waiting for them to leave. And then we get her and do her in the bar. Could still be read as a drug deal gone wrong."

De Boer nodded. "Boat waiting a mile away. And our men are out of there."

Thornton checked his watch. It was 8:01 p.m. "I'm sorry about Pieter, man."

De Boer nodded. "I've got the rest of my life to mourn him. But he's got a widow who doesn't know she's a widow."

"Jesus."

"She still thinks my brother is alive. I'll need to tell her all that when we get back. But first I want that fucker Nathan Stone deleted, and the girl."

Thornton said nothing.

"Are you okay, Craig? You've gone quiet on me again."

"I just want this over with. Fucking jinxed this whole thing."

Forty-Six

Stone was doing some breathing exercises as he stared at the stars in the inky sky, pondering what lay ahead for them that night. He had run the scenarios through his head a dozen times and still thought his plan was solid. He had to be careful, though. He didn't want his face popping up on any surveillance footage. He had gotten lucky so far. But he knew that even the best-laid plans could come apart at the seams.

He popped a couple of steroid-and-amphetamine pills, washing them down with a bottle of water. He tasted the bitter aftertaste, swallowing hard. He waited a few moments. Then he checked his watch. It was 8:19 p.m. precisely.

He waited until 8:20 and called Beatrice in Cudjoe. The phone rang three times before she picked up.

"Change of plan," he said.

Beatrice said, "Why?"

"I'm at a nice bar in Marathon," he lied. "Frank's Bar. Straight across the Overseas Highway from Big Pine Key. Overlooks the water. It's gorgeous."

"How far is that from where I am?"

"Thirty miles. Take Route 1 north. Forty minutes."

"Why so far away?"

"No reason. Cool little place I found."

She was silent for a few moments. He was worried she wasn't going to respond. "You still there?" he asked.

"Sure."

"Did you hear what I said? Change of plan."

Beatrice cleared her throat. "When do you want me to leave?"

"Leave right now."

"Right this second?"

"Yes. Drive straight here."

Beatrice sighed. "You're there already?"

"Yeah," he lied again. "Got a strong mojito. You like mojitos? I'll get one lined up for you."

"Sounds nice." Beatrice's voice betrayed nervousness.

"You okay?"

"I'm good. Just . . . I'm not good when plans are changed."

"Don't worry, I've got this."

Forty-Seven

De Boer took off the headphones he'd been using to listen in on the conversation between Stone and the woman. "What the fuck is he up to? Changing plans. Fuck!"

Thornton stared at the monitors. "I don't like it."

"It's almost as if he knows we're listening. And taking his bait."

Thornton clicked his fingers. "That's what it is. He's setting the bait for us."

De Boer stared out the side window. "You don't know that. You're overthinking it."

"Maybe. I hope so."

De Boer stared at the monitor showing the entrance to the beach house where the woman was staying. "Still no sign of her."

"He's doing the classic thing. He's setting a time and place to meet up. Then he changes it at the last minute."

"Then again, maybe we're making false assumptions. What reason would he have to think the phone in the house is being bugged?"

Thornton was quiet.

"Isn't it more likely that Frank's is just a bar in Marathon he likes and was always going to use, perhaps concerned that she might be compromised, maybe have gone to the cops?"

Thornton sighed. "Could be. I say we send one team up there now. Just to sit outside until we're all there. Observation only until they both leave, then we take them down."

"Fine." De Boer sent out the message that team A was to move from the bar in Big Pine Key and head up to Marathon. Stay in vehicle until further notice on arrival, he instructed.

"What about the No Name Pub?"

"We've still got your operatives in position. I say they stay as they are until further notice."

Thornton got on his cell phone and passed on that instruction to his team. "So we've got both places covered?"

De Boer took a few moments to consider the development. "Fuck."

"I know. It's like we're being played."

"It's either that or he's just unpredictable."

"We need to be on the ground in Marathon, or nearby, to make sure this fucker doesn't disappear again."

De Boer nodded. He glanced out the side window as the door to the house opened.

An operative's voice came through his earpiece. "We've got movement. She's on the move."

"Copy that. I want one car in front of her and one at a distance." De Boer stared at a monitor as the woman locked the front door of the beach house and walked over to the Jeep. He watched as she pulled away. He waited for a minute until she was out of sight. Then he cocked his head at Thornton. "Let's get in the SUV. Leave the van here just in case Stone decides to return."

Thornton climbed out the rear door of the van and got into the back of the waiting BMW SUV.

De Boer got in the front.

"Marathon?" said the operative who was driving.

"Frank's Bar."

They pulled away, leaving the white van with the two other operatives inside.

Forty-Eight

Berenger was in Sarasota watching dashcam footage from the BMW as de Boer and his guys finally closed in on Stone when his cell phone rang.

"Mark, plane waiting outside." It was Fisk.

"Sir, we're reaching the endgame here. I thought we—"

"You don't have to hang around for the endgame. I've seen the latest report. We're in a position to finally nail that fucker Stone. But I want you out of Florida and back with your family before the shit hits the fan down in the Keys."

Berenger took a few moments to contemplate what Fisk was getting at. "Sir, with all due respect, my work will only be done when Stone is neutralized."

"Mark, when's the last time you saw your family?"

"Quite a while ago."

"Months. So we're going to put this right. De Boer and his guys have this in hand."

Two men in suits appeared at a side door within the facility.

"Two of my people will accompany you back home," Fisk said.

Berenger stared at the men. "Those are your guys?"

"They work for me. They will make sure you arrive at your destination safely. Part and parcel of the contract."

"And you want me to go now?"

"The facility will be shutting down within minutes of Stone being taken out. I want you out of there. Out of sight. The Cessna is waiting."

Berenger thought the whole situation strange. "Sir, if it's all right with you, I'd rather just wait until I have confirmation that the job is done. It ain't over till it's over, as they say."

"You can't do any more. So, get on the plane, get out of there."

Berenger looked up at the footage showing de Boer and his guys talking in the car. "I've got some personal stuff I need to organize."

"We'll pack it up and ship it out to you. As of now you need to get on the plane and become a civilian again. You need to get out of Florida. The money all went into your account this morning."

"I saw that. I thought it was on completion."

"Mark, we'll talk soon."

"Shouldn't I say goodbye or something to the team here?"

"No. Your job is done."

The line went dead.

Berenger was accompanied out of the facility by Fisk's men. He turned to look around, and only the computer hacker brought in by de Boer looked up from his monitor. The kid nodded in acknowledgment.

A few minutes later he was in the air, headed to Iowa. As quick and as sudden as that.

Berenger was handed a whisky on the rocks. He tossed it back as the Cessna climbed through the night sky, the lights of Sarasota below.

He closed his eyes. He began to think of Nathan Stone at the mercy of de Boer and his crew. Finally, the end of the battle to track him down and kill him was in sight. He felt an emptiness in his soul despite everything, knowing Stone's life would soon be over.

Forty-Nine

De Boer opened up the iPad. It showed the BMW's GPS position, headed north through the Keys. "Okay, looks good. So, let's take this nice and easy. We've got people in position. And we're on her tail. But we need to keep at least a half-mile gap. No closer. Are we clear?"

"Got it," the driver said.

The miles rolled by as they headed on to Summerland Key and then Big Pine Key. From there it was Bahia Honda Key. Then Ohio Key and Missouri Key. Then on to the Seven Mile Bridge, which would take them up to Marathon in the Middle Keys.

He couldn't help but think of his brother. His tough brother. He would have to accompany Pieter's body all the way back to South Africa when the mission was complete. He knew his sister-in-law would have millions in her bank account as compensation. But that wouldn't mean anything to her. She was a widow now, raising the kids by herself in a gated community. He wondered if maybe his brother's family should move to his ranch for better protection.

De Boer stared straight ahead as the headlights illuminated the asphalt. His earpiece buzzed. "Kevin, we're in position in Marathon."

"Copy that. Any sign of the target?"

"We've scouted the bar, but nothing so far. We think he might've gone to the bathroom, but we're on it."

De Boer relayed the message to Thornton in the back seat. "They reckon he's in the bathroom. No escape for the fucker this time."

Thornton just stared out into the darkness, not saying a word.

"Don't go quiet on me again," de Boer said.

"Just thinking."

"About what?"

"About Stone. I'm wondering what Stone is doing now. Does he have one or two drinks under his belt? Is he relaxed? The annoying thing is that we'll have to go with a new game plan now. New bar, new location, and also, since Stone's there already, he might be able to check out the entrances and exits, have that covered."

"Yeah, but so will we."

"He's got us on our toes."

De Boer knew Thornton was right to feel uneasy. They were dealing with a highly dangerous operative. Unpredictable. Savvy. He pictured Stone kicking back with a beer alongside his mojito, having a piss before he met up with the girl. Perhaps making sure that the bathroom didn't have anyone in it. He wondered if there was direct water access from the bar. Was that something they needed to consider? He passed on his question to the team in Sarasota for them to come up with an answer. And fast.

His earpiece buzzed. "That was quick," he said. "Tell me about the water access."

"Our guys are looking into it. Meanwhile, I wanted you to know that Berenger got a call a few minutes ago and he's out of here."

"What?"

"I know. Strange."

"He took off? Seriously?"

"Two guys landed in a Cessna and escorted him to the plane. And that was that."

De Boer had expected Berenger, as the top guy, whom he reported to, to hang around. "Maybe a precautionary move before this goes down?"

"That's what I was thinking. We'll be cleaning up and getting out of here quick."

"Appreciate the heads-up, man," de Boer said.

De Boer ended the conversation. Ahead of them on the road was the woman in the Jeep. Stone was at the bar. De Boer chose to take Berenger's departure as a sign of confidence that things were finally going to plan. Then, just as they reached the halfway point on the deserted bridge, a siren blared behind them.

He glanced back and saw blue lights. "Are you kidding me?"

Thornton looked back, then turned to face de Boer. "All our IDs are fine. Relax, we're allowed to carry. We're good."

"I know. Just a fucking irritant, that's all. Pain in the fucking ass this whole job." De Boer looked back again as the cop started flashing his lights. "You think he wants us?"

The driver nodded. "Yeah, he's signaling for me to pull over."

De Boer sighed. "Fuck. Okay, do what he wants. No smart-ass comments. The guy's just doing his job."

The driver slowed down and pulled over. He adjusted his mirror, keeping an eye on the cop. "Yeah, he's taking a good look at our taillights."

De Boer glanced in the side-view mirror and saw the cop approach. He wore sunglasses and the uniform of the Florida Highway Patrol. His motorcycle was parked a few yards behind them.

The cop knocked hard on the window. The driver lowered it.

The cop was wearing forensic gloves. He smiled. Then he pulled an Uzi out and sprayed the vehicle with bullets until everyone was dead.

Fifty

Stone reached in through the window to unlock the car's doors. Then he rifled through the blood-spattered pockets of the three men in the SUV. He took all their cell phones. And it was clear that the guy in the front passenger seat had been giving instructions, sending operatives to the bar in Marathon where Beatrice was headed. He sent a text to Beatrice on the cell phone he'd given her. It read:

Drive past Marathon. Meet up where we first met.

Stone threw the Uzi into the blood-soaked back seat. He wanted the cops to think it was some drug deal or some gangland thing gone wrong.

He climbed back on Barney's old bike and gunned it across to Marathon. He found a deserted beach. He was careful to dump the Harley among the dunes and bury it with sand.

But first Stone pulled a backpack out of the pannier. Inside was a change of clothes. He took off the forensic gloves and bloodied cop clothes and buried them, then put on his clean clothes and switched the new cell phone on.

He walked a quarter mile, hot-wired a Toyota he found in a parking lot, and got back on the road, headed north, straight for Miami.

Fifty-One

Catherine Hudson was staring up at the big screens in the Miami office, struggling to comprehend the blood-spattered dashcam footage from the SUV that had been carrying de Boer and the other South African operatives. It was her worst nightmare. The whole operation had imploded. And still Stone and the woman were free.

When her cell phone rang, she nearly jumped out of her skin.

"Yes!" she snapped.

"You've got a problem." It was the harsh voice of Reg Thomson, the ex-SAS operative.

"What the hell happened?"

"Your men should've seen that change of time as suspicious. They must have had their doubts. But they were led to that location by that simple call. Staggering."

"How is that even possible? I can't understand this."

"I've been in the business for the best part of fifteen years, and I've never seen anything like this. Who the hell is this Nathan Stone? I mean, really, who the fuck is he?"

"Where are you now?"

"Watching things from my office here in Miami."

"What about your guys? Where are they?"

"One on a motorbike, two in a car, trailing Stone as we speak."

"Fuck!"

"I know. Complete, utter mess. It's a full-on clusterfuck. And you guys are rapidly losing control of this situation. Actually, I'll correct that, you've *lost* control of the situation. And it's going to head south from here."

"That's what you think?"

"You've lost the head of your operation. Stone has the rest of the team split up between three locations. And no one has a clue where he's headed or what he's planning."

Hudson closed her eyes. She felt as if she was losing her mind. The Commission—her brilliant idea—was in shambles, and their specially picked assassin, Nathan Stone, had spun so far out of their orbit of control it was beyond belief.

The more she thought about it, the more she wondered whether it was even possible to take out Stone and the woman without a blood-bath. How was this all going to end?

"Talk to me, Reg," she said. "How do we clean up this fucking mess?"

"I don't know if you or your guys have any idea what you're dealing with."

"Excuse me, I know exactly what we're dealing with."

Thomson sighed. "I didn't mean to snap at you. But this is not fucking good. And I don't think there are any good solutions to this. You need to let your superiors know. This is out of control. And you can quote me on that."

Hudson saw a light flashing on her desk phone.

"What do you want my guys to do?" Thomson said. "Your call."

"Look, keep tracking Stone, and we'll make the call on what needs to be done when it's time."

"And when will it be time? Let's get serious. We have a GPS fix on the car Stone stole. He's heading north, we think toward Miami, and so is the woman. So, that's something to work with. I think we should move a team into position in Miami to await instructions. How does that sound?"

"Do it." Hudson ended the call and picked up the desk phone. "Catherine speaking."

"I just got your message." It was William Black.

"It's a full-on nightmare scenario, sir. And it's not over. Not by a long shot."

"Catherine, in five minutes I'm meeting with the director and the chairman of the Joint Chiefs of Staff. And let me tell you, it's not going to be pleasant. So, I need answers. And I need to know the containment strategy."

Hudson glanced up at the screens. One was tuned to Fox News, which was now trumpeting breaking news in the Florida Keys. On the other screen, a police forensics team, visible on the dashcam, was photographing the sides and front of the SUV. "Shit, Fox is already on this."

"What?"

"Stone killed everyone in the vehicle. Kevin de Boer, all of them. Close range."

"Fuck."

"Sir, the time for containment has come and gone. Nathan Stone and the actress are both driving north on US 1, separately. Current GPS indicates Stone is two miles south of Key Largo. Next stop, Miami. You can count on it."

"He's clearly communicating with the actress. He's obviously given her a clean phone, untraceable."

Hudson sighed. "Possibly. Who knows? The fact of the matter is he will be heading to Miami."

"Why Miami?" Black asked.

"Good place to disappear. Bus, train, and plane hubs. And boats too. Nightmare. And we are failing to contain this."

"*You* are failing to contain this."

His tone sent a chill down her spine. "Sir, I'm taking full responsibility for this. Thomson's team is now, finally, on it," Hudson said.

"So was de Boer's."

Hudson sighed. "My take on this, sir, for what it's worth?"

"Please."

"I'd like Thomson and his guys to just take Stone out as soon as they can. On the street. Close range. In cold blood. And to hell with the consequences."

"Let's do it."

Fifty-Two

Stone dumped the car in a nondescript alley in South Beach, pulled on the backpack, and walked a circuitous route to the Deuce on Fourteenth Street. He was back in the bar where it had all begun. And it was like nothing had changed.

The Stooges were blasting out of the jukebox. A few stoners were loafing around the pool table.

Stone ordered a bottle of Heineken and a Bloody Mary. He knocked back the cold beer. It felt good. Actually, it felt fantastic. The adrenaline was still running through his body.

He stood and reflected on what had happened since he had first encountered Beatrice here. Neither of them could have foreseen what would transpire. He wondered whether she would turn up. Then again, he wondered if she wouldn't just head straight to the cops.

The Miami Beach police were only a few blocks away.

Stone didn't have to wait too long. Twenty minutes after midnight she strolled in, wearing sunglasses and smoking a cigarette. She stopped beside him, picked up the Bloody Mary, and knocked it back in one.

Stone ordered another round. "How you holding up?" he said.

Beatrice stared straight ahead. "Is it finished?"

Stone shrugged. "I sure as hell hope so."

She leaned in close for a moment. "You didn't think I'd turn up, did you?"

"I had my doubts."

The bartender handed over the beer and the Bloody Mary.

Stone clinked her glass with the bottle. "Got to hand it to you."

"What do you mean?"

"You're far tougher than I imagined. I misjudged you."

Beatrice shrugged. "Story of my life. Besides, I'm not buying that compliment. I was a terrified nutjob most of the time."

"You had your moments, that's true."

Beatrice smiled and shook her head. She looked over at the guys playing pool. "I'm terrified we're being watched."

"Relax."

"Easier said than done."

Stone gulped some more cold beer.

"Did that actually happen? Seriously? I'm trying to make sense of it. Shit, and this is where it all began. I'm having flashbacks."

Stone nodded.

"I mean, did that actually goddamn happen?"

"Keep it down," Stone said. He turned to the bartender and slid a napkin with a hundred-dollar bill under it across the bar. "That's for you. But I need a favor."

"Not a problem, man."

Beatrice said, "What's going on?"

Stone gave her a sideways glance. "Gimme a minute." He leaned in to speak to the bartender. "You smoke?"

"Yeah. Cigarettes, not weed."

"Same as me. Do you go out the back for a cigarette break?"

"Why do you need to know that?"

"Just humor me."

"Sure, that's exactly where I go."

"I need a favor. In return for that crisp hundred-dollar bill."

"What kind of favor?"

"Get a coffee and a cigarette and go out there."

"Now?" The guy frowned. "Why?"

"So you can tell me if there's anyone else in or around the alley. I mean any dudes hanging around, guys in cars, on motorcycles, whatever."

The bartender shrugged. "Why would you want to know that?"

"I'm a curious person."

"You're weird, my friend."

"Humor me."

"And if there is someone out there? What do you want me to do?"

"Take your time. Have your smoke and coffee. Then come back and tell me what you see."

The bartender was grinning. "Are you a cop? Is that it?"

"Like I said, I'm just curious."

"Okay, man, I'm in." The bartender slid the money into his pocket and disappeared out back.

Beatrice stared at Stone. "What the hell was all that about?"

"Just trying to get the lay of the land."

"You think we have a problem, don't you?"

"Just keep it down and keep it together."

When the bartender returned, he was flushed.

"You okay?" Stone said.

"Yeah . . ."

"So what's the story outside? Anything?"

The bartender nodded and leaned in close. "Two white guys in a car."

Stone processed the information. "Is that right? What kind of car?"

"A Suburban. Black. You know those guys?"

"What else?"

"One was talking into a cell phone."

"Passenger or driver?"

"Passenger."

Stone slid another hundred-dollar bill to the guy.

The bartender took a peek at the money. "Are you kidding me?"

"You did good. Thanks."

The bartender shrugged. "So what's that all about? Are they friends of yours? Is this a game you guys are playing?"

"It's fine. Just curious. Just keep it to yourself."

The bartender shook his head and smiled. "Whatever floats your boat, man." He drifted away from them to serve another customer farther down the horseshoe-shaped bar.

Stone whispered to Beatrice, "I need a favor."

"What kind of favor?"

He glanced over his shoulder toward the pool table, then handed her a twenty-dollar bill. "I'd like to see what you've got."

"I beg your pardon?"

"I mean, I'd like to see your acting abilities."

"Why?"

"I want you to go over to those guys shooting pool and ask to borrow their cell phone for a minute. Say your cell battery died. And give them the twenty. That's for their trouble."

"And why would I want to say that?"

"Just do what I say."

"There's something wrong, isn't there?"

"Just do it."

Beatrice looked at him long and hard. "Shit. I thought this was over."

"We might have some company."

"Where? Who?"

"Out back."

"Fuck."

"So I need you to do what I asked you."

Beatrice didn't hesitate. She slid off her stool, walked up to the guys shooting pool, and flung her arm around one of them.

Stone watched as she flirted with them before one handed over his cell in return for the twenty-dollar bill.

Beatrice returned to her stool and knocked back her drink. "What now?"

"I want you to call 911."

"Why?"

"Just do it."

"I don't like this."

"It is what it is."

"What does that mean?"

"It means they weren't there when we arrived ten minutes ago. Suspicious."

"You think they tracked us down? I thought it was done."

"Make the call."

"And what do I say?"

"Go into the women's bathroom, make sure there's no one there, and really give it everything you've got. I want you to sound frightened. And I want you to say there are guys with guns and drugs in a black Suburban behind the Deuce bar, Fourteenth and Collins Court. Got it?"

Beatrice nodded. "911. You sure?"

"Positive. Then hand the cell phone back to those guys."

Beatrice disappeared to the bathroom for a few minutes, handed back the cell phone, and sat down again. "Done. What now?"

Stone bought two more bottles of Heineken. He handed her one and clinked the bottle. "Well played."

She took a couple of large gulps and put down the bottle. It wasn't long before they both heard the blare of sirens in the distance.

Stone handed her the backpack. "I want you to leave the bar and get on a bus."

"Why? I just got here."

"Do it!"

"What about you? What are you going to do?"

"I'm going to deal with something. But I want you to get to safety."

"What's the backpack for?"

"Don't open it."

"Why?"

"Promise?"

Beatrice nodded. "Yeah, if that's what you want. I thought all this shit was over."

"It will be soon."

"So, I catch a bus? I don't understand."

"I'll call you on the cell phone I gave you within the hour. I want you to be on a bus headed to New York."

"I don't live in New York."

"Just do it."

"Where do I get a goddamn bus?"

"Downtown bus terminal. Catch a cab a block from here, outside the Flamingo Apartments."

"Okay. Then catch a Greyhound bus headed to New York?"

Stone nodded.

"What about you?"

"What about me?"

"What are you going to do?"

"Don't worry about me. Just get on a bus. And I will call you in an hour. Keep a close hold of the backpack."

"I'm scared."

"Do this and you're almost home."

"Promise?"

"I promise. Take care, Beatrice."

Beatrice smiled as she lingered for a moment. Then she got up and left the bar.

241

Stone finished his beer and ordered another. A minute later red lights seeped into the dark dive bar.

Stone signaled the bartender. "Can you do me another favor?"

"Sure thing."

Stone pointed at the bag behind the bar. "What's in that?"

"You crazy? Why do you want to know that, man?"

"Just curious."

"Gym gear. Workout clothes. Member of the Flamingo Park running club. I usually head on over after work."

"Five hundred dollars okay?"

"You kidding me? For a fucking gym bag?"

Stone nodded.

The barman grinned. "You're crazy. Are you a drug dealer or something? None of this makes any sense."

Stone slid the money to the bartender. "Tell me about it."

Fifty-Three

Catherine Hudson paced the secure office in Doral watching night-vision footage from the drone high up in the sky and adjusting her Bluetooth headset. The drone was currently above a black Suburban in an alley behind a bar. Miami Beach police were cordoning off the area.

Hudson's headset buzzed.

"Catherine?" It was Thomson.

"Reg, talk to me!"

"Two of my operatives are in custody."

"How did this happen? Or maybe I should rephrase that: How does this keep happening?"

"You tell me, Catherine. This is your baby, apparently."

"So you're blaming me?"

"Don't be so fucking touchy."

Hudson closed her eyes.

"One of my guys is still in the game. As soon as Stone leaves the bar, he's dead."

Hudson didn't say anything. She'd watched all her plans turn to dust before her eyes. They had one more roll of the dice.

"Do you copy that?"

"I copy that."

"We need to take him down now. We have to kill the fucker."

"You're sure your operative can handle it?"

"He's on a motorbike, line of sight to the bar entrance. We've already ID'd Stone. He's in the bar. Drone footage showed the woman leaving. We need to act. And quick."

Hudson was quiet as she contemplated this next move. It was so far from what the Commission should have been all about.

"The actress can be dealt with another day," Thomson said impatiently. "Stone is the number one target. I say we go into the bar and kill him point-blank."

Hudson began to pace the room. "How far away is the biker?"

"You need to green-light this, don't you?"

"Yup. Not in the bar. Outside, on the street. I want him to die like a dog."

Fifty-Four

Stone headed into the back office at the Deuce.

The bartender was waiting for him and shut the door. He handed over the Adidas gym bag.

Stone gave him a wad of notes.

The guy flicked through it. "Five hundred bucks! You've given me a thousand bucks in total! Are you kidding me?!"

Stone took the bag. "Thanks."

"Did you rob a bank or something?"

"Something like that." He glanced at the TV monitors. The security cameras showed cops combing the area around the black Suburban.

The bartender opened the door. "Two minutes, and you need to be out of here."

"Got it."

Stone closed the door and locked it from the inside. He unzipped the Adidas bag and pulled out the guy's gym gear. He stripped off his clothes. Then he pulled on the guy's white T-shirt, white shorts, matching trainers. Marled gray sweatshirt and sweatpants on top. He popped on some sunglasses.

He stuffed his backpack inside the Adidas bag and slung it across his body. He put the Glock in the elastic waistband of the sweatpants and pulled down the sweatshirt. Stone glanced in the mirror. He could be any guy headed to or from a South Beach gym. He adjusted the bag to conceal the gun down the back of his pants.

He took a deep breath.

Time to play, Nathan.

Stone unlocked the door and nodded at the bartender as he headed out of the bar. He turned right and headed down Fourteenth Street and past the cops, who had strung crime-scene tape across the alley. His senses were primed. He knew exactly what he was looking for.

He took a right on Ocean Drive and strode past a couple of drunken tourists arguing about baseball. Then he turned right up Thirteenth Street. His mind was thinking ahead. How it was all going to play out.

He walked for about half a mile in the heart of South Beach, past art deco hotels, apartments, art galleries, tattoo parlors, nail salons, and bars. He turned right on Euclid Avenue and walked a block until Fourteenth Street. Then he turned right and crossed over onto other side of the road. Then he crossed over at Washington.

Farther down the street, Stone saw a guy on a high-powered bike. Black leather, Ducati logos. He figured the biker was about a block down from the Deuce.

Stone could see that the guy had a perfect line of sight on everyone leaving or entering the bar. He must've seen Stone walking out of the Deuce. But since his clothes were different, he hadn't thought anything of it. At least Stone hoped that was the case.

Suddenly he felt as if a switch had been flipped in his brain. He was in the zone. Hyperaware of his surroundings. He began to walk down the street, coming up behind the biker. He felt crazier than he had for a while. Adrenaline coursing through his veins. His focus was the man on the bike. The guy was speaking into a yellow-and-black walkie-talkie.

Stone was getting closer. Fifty yards or so. Nearer and nearer.

He watched as the man put down the walkie-talkie. Perfect. He approached, unseen by the guy. He walked up to the biker and took aim. Then shot him in the neck. The guy collapsed to the ground, the bike crashing on top of him.

Screaming filled the humid air.

Stone stood over the biker and drilled two shots through the man's visor and into his gaping mouth. Pedestrians fled in all directions.

Stone picked up the bike, turned it around, and gunned it down the street, not bothering to look back.

Fifty-Five

Three minutes later, Hudson's cell phone rang. She stared at her computer showing the feed from the dead operative's crash helmet. She felt strangely disengaged, blood spilling into sight.

"Catherine, you need to get out of there," Thomson said.

"What?"

"My guy just got taken out. Didn't you see that?"

"Yes, I saw it. Of course. I'm watching it."

"That's why you need to move. Protocol."

"What the hell are you talking about? I don't answer to you."

"I'm acting on instructions from Black. I've got him waiting on the line to talk to you. Now!"

Hudson couldn't seem to get a handle on the nightmare that was unfolding. "The Director? I'm sorry, where are you?"

"Parking garage downstairs."

"Here?"

"Doral. Yes. So, you need to get out of there. And I've been tasked with getting you back home immediately."

Hudson closed her eyes, not knowing what to do. "Why doesn't the Director contact me directly?"

"Why don't you speak to him yourself? I've got him waiting on the line."

"What, now?"

"Right now. Better get a move on, don't keep him waiting."

Hudson's mind was racing. She quickly locked up and headed down in the elevator to the parking garage. She saw Reg leaning out of a silver Audi, signaling her. As she approached the car, she glanced in the back window. Sitting in the back seat were a woman and a swarthy middle-aged man wearing a black jacket.

Her blood ran cold. What the hell?

For a split second she was thrown by it all.

Hudson slid into the front passenger seat and buckled up. Thomson buckled up in the driver's seat.

Reg cocked his head toward the guy in the back seat. "This is one of my colleagues."

Hudson turned, but it wasn't to look at the man. She'd recognized the woman next to him from a photo she'd seen on LinkedIn. "What the hell is this, Becky? Thought you were State Department."

Hudson's old friend smiled sheepishly. "Sorry, there was no time. I was hoping to meet up with you and explain things. You probably guessed I'm not State Department."

"Yeah, I gathered that. So what's going on?"

Becky pointed to Reg, who was holding up a cell phone. "Boss is on the line. You might want to talk to him first."

Reg handed her the phone.

Hudson cleared her throat. "Sir?"

"Catherine . . . we thought it best to get you out of there while we can."

"Sir, this is most irregular."

"The events that have transpired are most irregular. We needed to act. I believe your old friend Becky is with you."

"Yes, sir. Would've been nice to be introduced earlier."

"That had been the plan."

"You knew about this?"

"Yes, I did."

Hudson was startled. He had misled her. But why?

"Becky will be joining your team. She will be working with you to clear this up."

"Working with me? Sir, with respect—"

"You've taken on a great deal, and I know you've had a hell of a time on this. We want to spread the load."

Hudson felt as if she'd been hit by a truck. She decided it was best, on reflection, to suck it up for the time being. "If that's what's deemed best, I can handle that."

"She's very good. She's worked in Europe for at least a decade."

"Doing what?"

"Trying to penetrate a foreign intelligence network within the UK. But I believe her skills could augment your own."

Hudson seethed. "I don't understand why we're getting out of Miami. What will that prove?"

"Listen, Catherine—"

"I know it's a terrible situation—"

"That's where you're wrong. This is not just a terrible situation. It's intolerable. And we need to take action. We need to secure our assets. In particular you."

"But I thought it was important to stick around until we tracked Stone down." Hudson glanced at Thomson, who was staring ahead as he drove onto the highway, headed north.

"Catherine," the Director said, "I can't have you compromised by being there while this all goes down. I don't want the Feds or police throwing up a dragnet and inadvertently pulling you into this mess. I can't have that."

Hudson could see that it made sense, no matter how tough a pill it was to swallow. "Sir, I'm sorry. I'm responsible for this."

"There will be a full debrief when you and Becky get back to see me. We're going to start fresh. New ideas. I'll talk to you in a few hours. Reg and one of his guys will accompany you and Becky on the flight."

"A flight to where?"

"We've got a facility not far from Orlando. We're assembling a new team to work on this around the clock with you."

"A new team? What new team?"

But Black was already gone.

It was surreal boarding the Gulfstream with Becky, Thomson, and the surly British operator, whose name she hadn't been told. Hudson and Becky made small talk during the bumpy flight. Becky knocked back two whisky and sodas and was deeply apologetic about not having been in touch and not being able to divulge her work. Hudson felt nauseous and popped a migraine tablet, washed down with a Diet Coke.

The Gulfstream touched down at an airfield nestled in some scrub twenty miles outside Orlando.

An SUV with tinted windows was waiting for them.

Hudson was shown to the passenger seat. Thomson got in the driver's seat as Becky got in the back, the man in the black jacket directly behind Hudson. She turned to Thomson. "So, where to now? I'm exhausted."

"Not far. A few miles from here. It's a nice facility. It's like a five-star hotel. You'll like it."

Hudson was surprised Reg knew about the secret facility. Had he been briefed by Black?

Thomson buckled up and glanced in his rearview mirror. "We all set?"

Becky's cell phone began to ring. "I'm sorry, this is a source of mine in London. I need to step out for two minutes to speak to her. Looks like an emergency."

Hudson rolled her eyes and sighed. "And this isn't? Sure. Whatever."

Becky got out of the SUV. Hudson watched her turn and walk back toward the Cessna, still parked on the runway. She felt uncomfortable as Thomson stared straight ahead.

He pulled out his phone. "Goddamn," he said.

"What?"

"Your boss wants to talk to me this fucking minute. This is getting ridiculous. I'll be right back." He got out the car, slamming the door behind him.

Hudson watched him disappear from sight in the rearview mirror, phone pressed to his ear.

There was a long silence before the guy behind her eventually spoke. His accent was well-educated English. "We'll find Stone, don't worry. We'll get that bastard. This is personal now."

Hudson turned around and smiled. "I'm sorry about that. Who was the guy on the bike?"

"An old friend of mine from my SAS days."

Hudson sighed. A few moments later Thomson returned, but he came around to the passenger side. She rolled down the window to speak to him.

"Your friend is being summoned back by the big chief," he said.

Hudson's head felt woozy; the migraine was worse than she thought. "What? Now? Are you kidding me? Seriously?" Her words echoed in her head as if she were underground. Her vision seemed strange too. In and out of focus. This wasn't the sort of migraine she usually got. "What the hell?"

Thomson shrugged. "Look, I'm going to smooth this out with Black."

"Yeah, do that."

He walked away and she rolled up the window.

Hudson looked in the rearview mirror. Everything was becoming fuzzier. She screwed up her eyes and thought she saw the Cessna door being shut. Slowly, the plane began to trundle down the runway. "What's going on? Are they leaving? Without me?"

The man in the back said, "Just getting the plane ready to take Becky back to DC, I guess."

Hudson felt as if her thoughts were congealing. She couldn't think straight. She began to feel strange. Sleepy. Then she felt sick. She watched the plane nearly disappear from view as it headed toward the far end of the runway, about a mile away.

"I don't feel well," Hudson said. Her eyes rolled back in her head. She tried to look around but couldn't. "I said I feel sick."

The man in the back was speaking to her, but the words were echoing, in slow motion. She felt as if she were sinking into a black hole.

Hudson's foggy mind tried to pinpoint what was wrong. And then it struck her. She had been poisoned. Or drugged. It had happened so quickly once she got into the car.

She began to panic.

Despite the swirling colors and shapes and forms merging and mingling into a terrible vision, she got some words out. "I think I'm going to be sick!"

The guy behind her loomed in her peripheral vision, as if checking whether she was okay. She glanced in the rearview mirror and saw Thomson on the phone as the plane took off in the background. It dawned on her that she was going to be killed. Drugged and killed.

Hudson felt a primitive fear grip her. Adrenaline raced through her body. She needed to run. Where? Anywhere. Now. "I'm going to be sick outside," she said.

She reached for the handle, flung open the door, and ran in a blind panic for the woods.

Hudson's first step on the tarmac got traction. She began to run. Faster than she'd ever run. She didn't look back. She just ran. She was a good runner. She was wearing sneakers. Thank Christ for sneakers.

Muffled shouts emanated from behind her. Echoing in her petrified mind. She heard more shouts. Reg. Screaming. Hollering.

Her breathing was all she could make out for a few moments. Her vision was fading in both eyes. Narrowing her view. Her sight was going.

She was in the woods. Trees. Tripping. She was being pursued.

"Catherine!" Thomson's voice was like a dark whisper in her head.

She stumbled again. She got to her feet, her legs wobbling. She began to cry. Colors and shapes merged and collided in her vision as she careened out of control. Heart pumping to the max. Breathing frantic. *Closing in. Need to escape. Think. Run. Escape.*

She slid through a muddy trail, tasting tears, feeling the drug in her system that was slowly but surely overpowering her. She needed to get to safety until the drugs wore off.

She stumbled through a brook and fell flat on her back. Mud and blood smeared her remaining vision. It was the same sensation as when a skiing accident had resulted in a detached retina in her left eye. Now she was feeling the same loss of sight in both eyes.

She got to her feet and immediately slammed into a low tree branch. Tasted blood. She fell again. Mud. Shouts behind her. Every second. Every second she needed to run. Until her heart burst.

The earth was shaking as she ran through the dark woods.

"Catherine!" The chilling voice of Reg's accomplice echoed around her. She sensed he was very close. "What's wrong, Catherine?"

She felt the men closing in. But she didn't dare look around. They were there behind her. Twenty yards away. Maybe less. Virtually on top of her. She sensed her life was coming to an end. *Fight! Fight, goddamn it!*

Up ahead she saw a chink of light through the twisted branches and foliage. She ran, panting, screaming, gasping.

Then she was skidding down a muddy embankment on her backside. The light was closer now and she ran toward it. Faster and faster. *Run! Faster. Don't stop!*

Suddenly, as if in slow motion, she tripped and her face smashed into gravel. She tried to lift her head, to see where she was, but blood smeared her vision.

Dear God in heaven, forgive me. Forgive me, Lord. Forgive them all.

For a moment her vision cleared, and Hudson realized in that split second where she was.

All alone, lying on a railroad track, a freight train coming straight at her. She closed her eyes, tasting tears, as she turned her head and took one final look up at the darkness, waiting and praying for the skies to open.

Fifty-Six

The sun was winking across the horizon when Stone left the crummy motel just south of Miami where he'd spent the night. He had ditched the motorcycle and the gym clothes but kept the Adidas backpack. He paid for the motel in cash and drove away in a car he had stolen a few hours earlier.

He headed south and dialed the cell phone he had given Beatrice.

"Hello?" Her voice sounded strong and clear.

"Where are you?" Stone asked.

"Some place in North Carolina, on the highway."

"North Carolina? Nice place."

"Is it? So, where are you?"

"Florida. Are you okay?"

"Okay? I'm fine. Alive. But I've been going out of my mind. You said you'd call in an hour. Why didn't you call?"

"Long story."

"Tell me about it?"

"I will."

"So, why did you want me to head to New York?"

"I wanted you out of Miami. And I needed you to drop off the grid for a little while. After you left, I neutralized one of the guys who followed us up from Key West."

Beatrice lowered her voice to a whisper. "Are you kidding me? You're killing again? When will this end?"

"It's over. For now. I promise."

"But I need to talk to my family. I need to be with them. I need to work. I need to live. I need money."

"I know all those things."

"So why the hell are you sending me to New York?"

"I want you to do me one last favor."

"Unbelievable. What kind of favor?"

"First, tell me: What part of the bus are you in?"

"I'm right at the back. I was going to try and get some sleep."

"Is there anyone near you?"

"Six seats away."

"Perfect. Now, listen to me very closely. Open the backpack, making sure no one sees you open it."

"Why?"

"Just do it. Careful. And have a look inside."

There was silence for a minute. Eventually, Beatrice came back on the line. "What the fuck is this?" she whispered.

"It's for you. It's for your family."

"Are you kidding?"

Stone felt his throat tighten. "No. I'm not kidding. It's yours."

"There's literally," she whispered, "goddamn hundred-dollar bills. Thousands of them."

Stone smiled. "I know."

"What the hell is this?"

"It's all yours."

"You're scaring me, Jimmy. What the hell is this?"

"It's yours. Keep it."

"It's blood money?"

"Some might call it that. I wouldn't. Neither should you. Don't look at it like that."

"Why? Why are you doing this?"

"Atonement."

"Atonement? Atonement for what?"

Stone sighed. "For everything I've done over the years."

"How much is in there?"

"Three million dollars. Nonsequential bills."

"Fuck off. Seriously? Are you fucking kidding me?"

Stone felt his grin widening by the second. "You've been to hell and back. For me it was just a bad few days."

"Why are you doing this? Is this a religious conversion?"

"Maybe. I don't know."

"How did you get so much money?"

"I've done a lot of bad things. And I've been paid a small fortune. I can't change my past. I can't change me. But I can change your life, and that's good enough for now."

"What are you going to do for money?"

"I've got money. Enough to get by on. Don't worry about that. Besides, I'm low maintenance."

Beatrice started to weep. "I just went to Miami for a goddamn audition."

Stone sighed. "I guess you got the part."

Beatrice sighed. "What are you going to do now?"

"Disappear for a while. What about you?"

Beatrice began to cry. "What about me?"

"What are you going to do?" Stone asked.

"I want to see my daughter. Maybe get us a nicer apartment. But I'm worried that *they* will be waiting."

"I don't think they will be."

"How can you be so sure?"

"It doesn't matter. It's over. And hopefully with that money you can start again."

Beatrice sniffed. "No one's ever been nice to me. No one. Why are you being nice to me?"

"We all need somebody, right?"

Beatrice said, "Jimmy . . ."

"By the way, my name's not Jimmy."

"It's not? But I've been calling you Jimmy since I met you."

Stone chuckled.

"Well I'll be damned."

"I hope you understand why I couldn't tell you."

"What is it? I mean, what's your real name? I'd like to know."

"Maybe one day."

"When?"

Stone sighed. "Beatrice, is that your real name?"

"Yeah."

"Beatrice, it's been a blast."

"It sure has."

"Maybe we'll meet up again one day. Then I'll tell you my real name."

Beatrice sobbed and laughed at the same time. "Jimmy, or whatever your name is, I'd like that. That'd be nice."

"You take care," Stone said, and hung up.

Epilogue

Three days later, William Black was staring out of the window of a Cessna en route to Kabul when the phone on the armrest rang. He picked up the secure line. "Black," he said.

"Sir, I was told to call you." The voice belonged to CIA officer Becky McFarlane.

"Thanks for calling back. How are you settling in?"

A deep sigh. "I'm settling in fine, sir."

"Becky, I'm sorry we're talking in such circumstances. This must be a very trying time for you. I know you two were close in college."

"We were close in college. But we lost touch."

"Catherine . . . Terrible way for her to go."

"I'm struggling to wrap my head around it, sir. She was the last person in the world I'd expect to take her own life. She was always so focused. She didn't seem suicidal at all."

"Becky, I've got to be up front with you. Catherine had, unbeknownst to any of us, an addiction to a prescription painkiller for an old knee injury."

"I see."

"This is just between us and not to be shared with her family. She was also taking antidepressants. A lot of antidepressants were found in her system, according to the medical examiner. Toxicology tests are showing signs she was using a drug used to treat epilepsy."

"Epilepsy?"

"No history of that at all. So, we've got a cocktail of drugs in her system, and I've just been told that she had consulted a psychologist in Arlington. She revealed that Catherine had talked of suicidal thoughts."

"Oh my God. If only we'd known. I feel so bad that I had to fly back. And to think that I was one of the last people to see her. What exactly happened?"

Black wasn't going to get drawn into a conversation. "We should have spotted some of the signs. But her line of work was very isolating, not being able to divulge her work to her family, the whole strain of it, and the disintegration of her pet project, it's all very sad."

"She seemed pretty touchy when I spoke to her in the car before the flight. Even the couple of calls I made to her. But I had no idea she was suicidal."

Black sighed. "I thought the world of her."

"I was thinking of perhaps paying my respects at the funeral."

"I think under the circumstances it would be best to allow her family the space and time to come to terms with this."

"I understand."

"Becky, I'm out of the country and I've got a videoconference call in an hour. So I need to talk business."

"Sir?"

"I want to talk about your new role. This wasn't how I had imagined you joining the team a few weeks back. But we are where we are. We think it is imperative that all Catherine's work and vision don't go to waste. The truth of the matter is her idea . . ."

"The Commission?"

"Her idea was a great one. But she wasn't served well by some of the people on her team. But those people are gone, and that's neither here nor there. The fact of the matter is that you now have the responsibility of tracking down Nathan Stone."

Acknowledgments

I would like to thank my editor, Jack Butler, Jane Snelgrove, and everyone at Amazon Publishing for their enthusiasm, hard work, and belief in the new American Ghost thriller series. I would also like to thank my loyal readers. I'd also like to thank Faith Black Ross for her terrific work on this book. Special thanks to my agent, Mark Gottlieb, of Trident Media Group, in New York.

Last but by no means least, my family and friends for their encouragement and support. None more so than my wife, Susan.

About the Author

J. B. Turner is a former journalist and the author of the Jon Reznick series of conspiracy action thrillers (*Hard Road*, *Hard Kill*, *Hard Wired*, *Hard Way*, and *Hard Fall*), as well as the Deborah Jones political thrillers (*Miami Requiem* and *Dark Waters*). He loves music, from Beethoven to the Beatles, and watching good films, from *Manhattan* to *The Deer Hunter*. He has a keen interest in geopolitics. He lives in Scotland with his wife and two children.